NEW
TOMORROWS

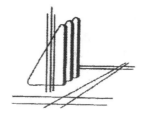

NEW TOMORROWS

New Beginnings Beyond Old Endings

Don C. Davis, ThB, BA, MDiv

Archway Publishing books may be ordered through booksellers or by contacting:

Archway Publishing
1663 Liberty Drive
Bloomington, IN 47403
www.archwaypublishing.com
1-(888)-242-5904

Cover inspiration by Nolan Davis

ISBN: 978-1-4808-0889-8 (e)
ISBN: 978-1-4808-0890-4 (sc)
ISBN: 978-1-4808-0888-1 (hc)

Library of Congress Control Number: 2014914752

Print information available on the last page.

Archway Publishing rev. date: 2/5/2015

ACKNOWLEDGMENTS

A Place In the Story is the best of positive future-vision fiction, inspired by successful achievers.

Inspiration has come from multiple sources, but none greater than from my wife, Mary, and our sons, Charles and Nolan, and their families. Mary, whose own success story continues to inspire her family, has been my devoted supporter and skillful editor. Along with these, there is the continuing influence of having parents who were good people.

The overview nature of my books has come from a list of writers whose books and articles explored the future, advanced knowledge, shared their knowledge base from science and technology, inspired positive insights, and led the way to a knowledge-based faith.

Those who have had a major influence on my thoughts and paradigms include: Norman Vincent Peale, Napoleon Hill, Albert Schweitzer, Og Mandino, Carl Sagan, Norman Cousins, Bill Gates, Fulton Oursler, Dale Carnegie, Theodore Gray, Norman Doidge, Martin E. P. Seligman, Michio Kaku, and others, whose vision is a reference to the future more than to the past.

From these, I have gathered an overarching view of the future. Like an impressionist painting, these provide a bigger picture of our place in the story of the new sacred.

To: Dr. James Kelly *james/mariakelly@crx.com*

From: Steve Kelly *stevekelly@crx.com*

Dear Granddad,

It was a special moment for me when I heard you speak at the Young Writer's Conference at the university today. When you came to the platform to speak, I leaned over and proudly whispered to my class-mate, "That's my granddad."

It's not every day that a college student can attend a Young Writer's Conference where his granddad is the featured speaker. But, as a leading-edge thinker and metaphorical writer, you were the perfect choice.

As I sat there listening to you, I had a grand idea. You said that you were working on a new book of metaphorical stories. I thought, what if granddad would be willing to tell the stories he is writing in his new book to his grandchildren while he is writing them.

We all loved to listen to the stories you told us on the porch at the farmhouse, when we were all children. All of us are young adults now, but I kept adding to my idea. Even though you live in town and come out to the farmhouse only as a retreat, and to write, we could all come together on the porch at the farmhouse in a kind of story seminar, and you could tell us the stories you are writing for your book. Would you consider that?

You have been, not only an esteemed minister, practical philosopher, professor, and author, but a much loved granddad. You have followed your grandchildren's college days and young careers with special in-terest. Because of your interest in all of us, I am daring to make this special request.

So I have come to the dorm, following your presentation, to write this email. What I hope is that you will say, "Yes."

E-mail me back at your convenience.

Your grandson,

Steve

To: Steve Kelly *stevekelly@crx.com*

From: James Kelly *james/mariakelly@crx.com*

Dear Steve,

I received your e-mail and am so very pleased that you have come up with what I think is a wonderful idea.

The answer is an immediate, "Yes." I would be honored. It would be a privilege for me far above speaking at the writer's conference where you began your idea. Maybe all of you could give me some good feedback as I finalize these stories. Having my grandchildren as a focus audience would add an important dimension to the stories. Of course, you know me, the stories would be quite metaphorical and in a fiction genre. Beyond that, I would want to add in some serious philosophy out of my own journey stories. So, yes indeed, I would be willing to tell my stories to all of you!

Summer is near and the kudzu along the edge of the porch, with its delightful fragrance, will be in full bloom. I welcome the opportunity to share. And, I might add, your grandmother will be thrilled to have all of you at the farmhouse at the same time.

So, Steve, go ahead with your plan. Work out a time with all seven of your cousins and let me know any way I can help. Be sure to include my two newest "grandchildren," since Brian is married to Linda, and Marsha is married to Wilson. Be sure to include Linda and Wilson.

Granddad

CHAPTER ONE

Outside Eden

Living on the growing edge of the future instead
of the holding edge of the past.

GRANDMOTHER'S KITCHEN AT THE FARMHOUSE HAD BEEN A FAVORITE gathering place for the whole Kelly family many times. All members of the family were always so very welcome to come out to the farm at any time, but today was the time Granddad was privileged to tell stories just for his young adult grandchildren.

The aroma of fresh baked cookies filled the whole farmhouse. As each of the grandchildren arrived, and after hugs and excited greetings in the den and kitchen, and sampling Grandmother's cookies, they all gravitated to the porch. Kudzu wound its way along the edge of the porch through the banisters and decorative grids on the posts. The fragrance of the kudzu blossoms filled the air, just as Granddad had said. Granddad joined the progression out to the porch and sat down where Steve had placed a special chair at the bend of the porch for him. The grandchildren slanted their chairs toward Granddad and waited in eager expectation.

Granddad crossed his legs at the knee, placed his hands on the arms of his chair, and looked admiringly at his select waiting audience. His voice was pleasant and mellow as he began. "I am a storyteller, teacher, metaphorical philosopher, and an adventurer into tomorrow. I am an explorer in the oneness of all existence. This farm, with its towering trees, open fields, winding roads, grassy meadows, and rippling branch stream, is my "Walden Pond". It's here I see the world more clearly, gain perspective on the on-going human story, and envision my privileged place in the story. But right now, I am a granddad who is so honored by you, my grandchildren, that I can hardly believe what is happening. So, thank you, Steve, for your beginning dream that has led to this high privilege. And thanks to all of you for making this little story seminar possible by being here at this favorite place. This is one of the greatest honors of my life. It's a real challenge that I welcome. I have to jump across the years from when I told stories to you as children to tell them now, not just to you as young adults, and I say proudly, but to the leading-edge thinkers you have become.

Of course, I am not just a storyteller. I am a storyteller who is trying to lift our human identity to a higher level. Stories are carriers of identity. They become a kind of parallel passage, in which we define who we are and plan to be, and what we plan to give to life as our story. That, in turn, becomes our ongoing bargain with life. Stories allow us to create our own pathways of imagination that define how we can live in our digital-molecu-lar-cell phone age as positive explorers into new tomorrows. We need farmhouse porches for new dreamland. It's where we can put the past behind us and the future before us. It's where we can turn old endings into new beginnings. So, while we must face the realities of how things are, we must never accommodate ourselves to them so much that we loose the ability to look ahead and see what can happen when we follow the possibilities generated by our dreams."

Granddad looked out through the kudzu as though he were peering into a distant yesterday. Or was into tomorrow he was seeing? Ending the glance away, he turned back to his little porch audience and said, "The first story I want to tell is the Garden of Eden story, where old endings were also new beginnings.

There are thousands of views overlaid on the old story, including my own. So right upfront, let me tell you that I look back on the old story through glasses colored by a modern day understanding of the progression of our human story which respects the molecular nature of all existence. We humans are a very special combination of atoms in their molecular arrangements, which has been passed along to us through our DNA. One of the special characteristics we inherit in our DNA is the ability to choose, and redirect our own brain signals. We program and reprogram our lives by the way we think.

This old farmhouse porch has heard a lot of stories. It's time for us to add some of our own. As we do, let me raise one little, but important, flag. It's so easy only to reconstruct yesterday, rather than create tomorrow. That becomes a serious roadblock. My hope is that together, we can create tomorrow. So my stories are about identity which leads to the next level up for a place in the story in new tomorrows.

Even as I retell classic stories, I must tell them in such a way that they align with the best science that we know, which is constantly being updated. It is necessary, therefore, to cross a great divide from an authority-based world view, over to a knowledge-based paradigm. It's a transition from a transcendence base for human identity to a self-development view, where the future we envision and the choices we make are up to us and become our request of life. It's the new sacred.

Now that we are experiencing the obsolescence of traditional authority-based religion, we need to build something of even greater promise. I believe it is time to build an identity based in a knowledge-based faith, informed by science and technology, and the Big Ten Universal Qualities. If this framework of identity defines the persons we seek to become, we will build a noble future that we can be proud to claim as our new tomorrows story.

We have shared enough parallel journey as you were growing up that I know your faith paradigms are open-source, that you keep adding insight. So the stories we share here on this old porch will simply be an upgrade in a faith that respects the molecular nature of all existence, and our place in an overarching infrastructure of ideas. All of this will be reflected in my story about the Garden of Eden and its representative people, Adam and Eve. It raises a question: What if no one ever challenged assumptions?

In the dewy dawn of civilization, the awakening of human consciousness, and a time when mythology was the way people saw the world, a storyteller from long ago told a story of how it all began.

After God made the stars, sun, moon, and earth, he came down to earth and planted a garden in a fertile valley. He planted lots of trees, especially fruit trees. From time to time, he came to see the trees as they grew. He especially loved to come when the springtime sun had warmed the air and the fruit trees had begun to bloom and scatter their pink and white petals in the wind.

It was even more special when he came in the summer and saw the delicious figs, peaches, pears, plumbs, and apples, just ready to be picked. That's when he wanted to have someone like himself, with whom he could share this delightful garden of plenty. He knew it was time now for him to make someone to live here all the time to take care of the garden and enjoy the fruit. So he took some of the clay from the earth and made a man and a woman, Adam and Eve, and breathed into them life like his own. They could live here in the garden and be a part of the delights and wonders of the Garden of Eden.

When God came to visit, they enjoyed walking along the pathways in the garden, smelling the flowers, listening to the birds, and eating some of the delicious fruit. Then one day God said, 'I like for you to enjoy the fruit here, but there's one tree in the garden from which I don't want you to eat any of its fruit. See it right over there.'

'Why not?' Eve wanted to know.

'It's bad for you,' God said, 'and if you eat some of that fruit, you will die.'

Eve said. 'I don't know what that means, but there's plenty here without it.'

But one day, as she walked near that tree, and stood admiring it's symmetrical limbs and green leaves, with fruit hanging down from every limb, she heard a voice speaking. She didn't bother to look around, just kept admiring the tree.

'Why don't you eat some of that beautiful fruit?' the little voice said.

'Oh, no.' Eve said, 'God said that if we ate any of that fruit we would die.'

'Really?' the voice said. 'You think God really meant that? Well, that's not quite the way it is. On the contrary, if you eat some of that fruit you will become wise, like God. No wonder he doesn't want you to eat any of it. Besides, he certainly wouldn't kill you now that he has made you, would he?'

Eve turned around to look. All she saw was a serpent slithering away in the grass. She turned back and just stood there looking at the tree. 'Looks good, doesn't it,' she said to Adam. 'Why don't you try some?'

Adam responded quickly, and with a coy smile. 'I'm not going to try it. You try it.'

'Well, I'll do just that, and find out what the real story is,' Eve said, as she reached up and plucked a red delicious apple from the tree. When she took that first big bite, the sweet juice oozed around the side of her mouth. 'Oh, my,' she said. 'It's gooood. It's delicious!' She reached up and picked another one of those beautiful apples and handed it to Adam. 'Here. Try it. You'll like it'

So Adam took a big bite, while Eve continued to bite into her apple in big chunks. "Good, isn't it?" she said. 'I don't see anything wrong with these apples.'

They walked on through the garden, munching away at their apples, right down to the core. That's when they saw God walking down by the creek, and coming their way.

'God won't like it if he sees us eating fruit from the forbidden tree,' Eve said. 'Quick, throw that core away and act like nothing ever happened.'

'Better still,' Adam said, 'Let's hide in the bushes so he can't find us.'

Quickly they hid behind some bushes. But God just kept coming their way, right up to where they were. They had no choice but to step out and say, 'Good afternoon, God. Pleasant day, isn't it?'

'Surely is,' God said, 'A wonderful day! But why were you hiding from me? Didn't you want to see me? Tell me. Have you eaten some of that fruit I warned against? Is that it? You don't have to answer. I already know. And you may know how very disappointed I am. You have not been an obedient steward of the garden the way I asked, so I can't let you stay here. You have to leave. Go find your own garden to take care of. You don't belong here any more.' Then God walked away.

Immediately two angels came and led Adam and Eve out of the garden, through the gate, and closed the gate behind them. Adam and Eve looked back. The two angels were standing there, guarding the gate.

Slowly Adam and Eve walked away, down the hill, and down to the valley near the creek. 'Guess we will just have to start our own garden,' Eve said. 'How about here near where the creek empties into the river? Maybe we can find some stones to put across the creek to back up the water and make it deep enough to swim in after we have been working in our new garden all day.'

'Fine with me,' Adam said. 'We'll just consider the gate that went closed behind us, to have become a gate opening before us.'

And with that, they put an old ending behind them and a new beginning before them."

Granddad looked at his grandchildren on each side. With a sneaky little smile he said, "And it's on that side of the gate where all of us live and work – outside Eden.

But, why was Eve not supposed to eat fruit from that one tree? Was it not about the quality of the fruit at all, but a test of their identity – who they really were? They had been given choices, but what did that freedom mean? Were they truly free to make choices and test results, or were they bound by authority? They could never know what that freedom of choice meant until it was tested – until they went beyond safety zones and defied needless limitations. The boundaries in their minds were limitless and they had to explore beyond these old boundaries if they were ever to find who they were on new frontiers of experience and knowledge. That was the wisdom they could have – a wisdom born out of inquiry and exploration in a real world.

It was a contest between being locked in by authority, and the freedom to make choices in open-ended knowledge. So, here we are now, exploring new pathways of thought and testing who we are, not only in our respective garden world, but from which we send out instruments of exploration, beyond the borders of earth, into the expansive distances of the moon and planets, stars and galaxies. And here, in our laboratories we are exploring the components of cells, and learning to make new ones. These macro and micro explorations have thrust us into a new age of enlightenment which can be part of our gardens where we test the limits of who we are.

And here we are, today's, Adam and Eve, listening to an old story, retold for new explorers who are expanding inquiry with leading-edge new questions about ourselves. It's the ongoing spirit of Eve on new metaphorical journeys.

First, let's ask, metaphorically, of course, why did Eve really want to taste that fruit so much? Was it because she wanted to be wise and be like God? And, does the more we learn and know, make us more like God? And, is that so bad, to want more understanding of how everything really works? Is that why you wanted me to tell you my stories, so we could explore together? In any case, our best perspective is not just to look back on yesterday, but to be sure we look ahead at tomorrow. That search itself is an extension of the creative spirit of Eve and deserves a place in the continuing story of the Adam and Eve that we all represent.

So look around. Look where we are. Look through the kudzu, down into the valley there. The person who tends the farm has just rolled up many big bales of grass hay. There is a little instrument on his tractor that receives a digital signal from his computerized baler, telling the tractor when to stop so it can wrap the hay with string and then kick the big new bale out. This current level of digital technology represents the progression of many years of searching and innovation, through which we are advancing new technologies and engineering to new levels of usefulness.

And look at us. Even though your grandmother retired a couple years ago from teaching in the public school, she is still teaching as a volunteer, helping children with learning disabilities, learn to read, still tasting apples in new ways. I have chosen to continue teaching at the university, even though it is a recurring course which springboards out of my writing. In addition, I am privileged to teach a class of young adults at church about faith and success philosophy. I've been invited to speak at an interdisciplinary conference of ministers, doctors, lawyers, scientists, and writers. And that's a real challenge. But I see all this as a chance to taste the apples of new inquiry at new levels. So maybe that's what is really going on here on this old porch where we are now – tasting apples, testing limits, and defining identity, outside Eden.

But more especially, look at yourselves. Look at who you are, and the ways you are tasting apples.

Steve is still in college, and working toward a degree in environmental science. Now that's tasting apples in new gardens, outside Eden. Of course, he's just now getting deeply into it as a junior.

Sue is in real estate, and the one who cherishes this farm and farmhouse most, though I am warning her, and all of you, too. You must never sell this place. Keep it as one of the treasured places where any of you can gather for fun, reflection, memories, and to explore the wonders of nature. It can be a special family retreat, where you may invite your grandchildren some day and reflect on the pathways you have traveled since this day - your 'Walden Pond.' Let it represent the better human side of our identity in an age that is increasing the techno-human aspect of our future.

Norman is a computer systems engineer. He's the one all of us call when we are having problems with our 'digital apples.'

Mel is with UNESCO, an acronym for United Nations Educational, Scientific, and Cultural Organization. He travels a lot, and he's the one Steve had to work with most to make this schedule fit so we could all get together here at one time.

Les teaches physics at a nearby college, where teaching physics is only part of what they hope students will learn there. They want their students to have an understanding of where we are in our time, which overarches math and science, religion and philosophy, so that we understand the molecular oneness of all existence, and, in turn, build our lives on the better side of our humanity.

Brian works in the admissions office at the university where I am privileged to teach. He works at an important entry point for new eras of learning. He is smart, smart enough to choose to marry Linda, who is a delightful addition to this circle of grandchildren. The second graders Linda teaches are so very fortunate to share her positive enthusiasm for life. And so are we.

Marsha is the oldest one among you. She's the little girl we doted over first as grandparents. She has her own art studio and business. Her paintings are visionary. Her paintings do what we are trying to do here — link yesterday to new tomorrows to create a future vision of marvel and surprise.

Anyone can see that Marsha is not just older, but wise, too. She talked Wilson into marrying her. I tease, of course. They met in college and became instant friends. They still are.

Wilson sells computer systems for large business operations. I see him and Norman talking together. They seem to know what each other is talking about. I don't. I just want them to keep my laptop working.

But who are we, beyond all these niches into which we are trying to fit in an info-tech world? Here we are, trying to see if the stories of yesterday can inform today and tomorrow in ways we can extend the inquiring spirit of Eve. Our big opportunity, then, is not to defend the past, but define the future. It's an opportunity to integrate the progression of our human story with our growing knowledge base of science and technology, and the Big Ten Universal Qualities, so we can enter a bold, wholesome, honorable request of life.

We tend to think of time as linear. Adam and Eve couldn't have stayed in that garden forever anyway. Maybe they needed a good reason to leave early, an exit from servility to authority, out to where they could find their way to new challenges, out to where they could grow, not just a new garden, but a new Adam and Eve.

If we dare to listen, we can hear Eve speaking through the language of her apple-tasting action. What's that old phrase, "What you do speaks so loud I can't hear what you are saying?" Through what Eve did, we can hear her speaking, asking, "Am I to be guided by untested authority, or should I be guided by acquired knowledge, born out of using my greatest power given to me — the power of the mind and its ability to think ahead and make choices? Must I not dare to go on beyond unthinking surrender to authority, with no better explanation than the threat and fear that I will die?"

Nothing exists without change — without old endings becoming new beginnings. Living forever in a frozen state is not even desirable. What is desirable is to be a person of choices, where what we choose has consequences.

Because so many have used the old apple-tasting story as a reason to surrender in fear and be subservience to authority, that makes it important to listen to Eve speaking through her actions to expand the spirit of inquiry and test all that happens in the real world in which we live. It's this daring spirit that lets us arrive at where we are in our new molecular age, where the future we ask for becomes our request of life. So, let her speak, to, and for us! Let her speak of the courage needed to integrate the best of our universal qualities, and the best of our science and technology into each other so that we get as close as we can to planting our garden of dreams for a wise sustainable future for our human family.

Inside or outside Eden, all Adam and Eve had, was a place in the story. And that's all any of us ever have — a place in the story. It may be that this old porch is a little piece of our place in the story, where we can remember the past, but explore the future, as a new garden, and new sacred ground.

Perhaps Eve was wrong in her defiance of rules, but she was not wrong to press the unexplored side of unanswered questions, where new knowledge can lead to creative ventures for new tomorrows. She was right, there should be a restless discontent which drives any of us to cross untested limits and explore new opportunities for knowledge and wisdom. Unless one pioneers beyond limiting boundaries, they will become a new wall in whatever the extended garden is for any of us. Almost everybody who accomplishes anything of worth has to push beyond lesser prohibitions to honor higher obligations and new possibilities.

Adam and Eve had the freedom to make choices. They could choose between being imprisoned by their fear of death and subservience to a God whose commands would have paralyzed their creativity, or they could choose to push back the edge of the possible even if they had to plant their own garden. Yes, of course we die, whether we taste the apple or not. Everything dies. It's part of the cycle of life from birth to death. But what about choosing to live before we die? Shall we live within yesterday's limits, or shall we create new frontiers where we push back the edge of the possible?

Eve took risks which landed her in the information age, in the science and technology age, in the molecular age. Having the freedom to make choices, she represented researchers exploring the molecular nature of micro existence with the Large Hadron Collidor. She represented the scientific research of J Craig Venter to cross boundaries in cell behavior and create synthetic life, and new choices. She represented astronomers using the Hubble Telescope, and its successor, the James Webb Space Telescope, to extend inquiry to the distant edges of space. She represented those who listen for God to speak in new languages, in new garden places.

So, none us are set by the mythological beginning couple so much as informed by their story about how to push back the edge of the possible and turn old endings into new beginnings – how to live creatively in new gardens we can make for ourselves.

Look at some of our new gardens we are creating, as open gates before us. Look at our schools and universities. We all owe so much to them for creating new pathways of knowledge. Look at our research centers. Look now beyond even the Hubble Space Telescope, or the Large Hadron Collidor in Geneva, Switzerland – look at the ventures into the edge of space being carried out now by Richard Branson, Jeff Bezos, and other billionaire entrepreneurs, who not only take us up to the edge of space and beyond, and who are testing who we are in whatever our respective space may be. Look at what is happening in nanotechnology. Look at what is happening in regenerative medicine, pioneered by Dr. Anthony Attala. The list goes on, as we reference the multiple new developments which are a part of science and technology, and which make it important that we update our religion, our philosophy, and our identity so that we see and measure ourselves, not only by who we have been, but by who we can be in a new and better garden. Does not all this give us a place in the story where we need to close the gate on yesterday, so we can open the gate on tomorrow?

I know, when we began this metaphorical exploration, any one of you could have pointed to the chaos in the world family and raised serious questions. There are so many travesties in our world that it's hard to believe people could be as bad as some are. While we dare not close our eyes to the problems around us, and the problems we face, we can choose to see in them some kind of opportunity to work for something better. We can look for ways to turn old endings into new beginnings wherever we may be on our journey story.

I am so pleased that I can refer to the professions you have entered upon. I see these as your new beginnings in a brand new world of hope and promise. I could call any one of you, Adam, or Eve, planting your leading-edge new gardens, outside Eden.

Outside Eden. That's where we are – always outside Eden. It means seeing the open gate before us, as more important than the closed gate behind us. It means seeing what we have, instead of what we have lost. It means living on the growing edge of the future instead of the holding edge of the past.

Outside Eden means doing the best we can in far less than ideal circumstances. It means believing in ourselves beyond other people's doubts. It means giving our best in spite of disappointment, injustice, setbacks, or loss. It means reaching beyond every failure for one more chance at success.

Outside Eden means that we will always work in less than ideal circumstances. We will face real hardships, adversity, injustice, and challenge. But it also means that we won't give up just because the world is not perfect and the way is difficult. When we struggle from our cocoon stage, that is when we arrive at new beginnings, where part of any achievement is the reach itself.

Outside Eden means believing in ourselves and our own new tomorrows in spite of error, wrong decisions, or anything else that pits us against surprising new challenges. Our greatest fulfillment is always beyond some gateway of difficulty and the promise of the future is to be found as we are testing new limits – as we are Eve and Adam.

CHAPTER TWO

I See Rainbows

Whatever the size and scale of our floods, our
rainbows need to be dream size.

FOLLOWING A LUNCH BREAK, GRANDMOTHER HELPED LAUNCH THE next session by bringing out a pitcher of tea and cookies. Just placing them on the table was an invitation for all of them to help themselves and to say "Thank you" to their beloved grandmother.

Granddad spoke gently as he said, "I greatly appreciate, and have enjoyed, the engaging discussion we shared following the garden story, and I am so pleased to see the level of dialogue among all of you, with your new generation perspectives. But for the moment, we can put that on pause so we can incorporate another story into our imagination, metaphors, and discussion. Let me tell you about a man who saw rainbows.

In the early dawn of civilization, a story teller told a legendary and metaphorical story about a visionary man who was building a most unusual boat. When we listen imaginatively, we can hear the wooden hammer-strokes, as this man was hard at work, high on the bow of a big boat he was building. His name was Noah. He was building an ark to launch himself and his family on the other side of a great flood, which he believed was coming soon.

Listen. Wham! Wham! Wham! Gradually the wooden pegs were squeezed into the holes. Down below we can hear some of his neighbors, as they scoffed and made fun of him and his big boat. 'Have you ever seen anything like that in all your life?' one of them asks sarcastically.

'Never!' another responded. 'Nobody has ever needed one of those things, whatever it is. And you can be sure of something else, nobody is going to need one of them for a long, long time, for it is never going to get from here to the river. And he dares to call it a boat.'

'Hey, Noah,' one of them yells out.

The hammering stops.

'Noah, we want to know something. How are you ever going to get your boat, or whatever it is, from here to the river?' A roar of cynical laughter rises from the group.

The hammering begins again. Wham! Wham! Wham!

But it wasn't just a boat Noah was building. He was building a bridge to carry the human family beyond an age of evil into a new age of hope and promise.

Watch the storm clouds gather and see the lightning flash. Listen as the thunder crashes and rumbles. Watch Noah, as he hurriedly gathers animals and leads them up the long gangplank, with the usual difficulty it takes to get a goat to follow, or be dragged. Watch Noah and his family as they are the last to go inside the ark. Listen as the door slams shut, with help from the wind! Hear the pelting of the first big raindrops on the wood shingles of the roof. The ark is ready to launch Noah and his family on the other side of a big storm.

The rain lasts for days and days. The water begins to rise in the creeks, and to cover the low lands. The boat begins to float as the water gradually creeps up the sides of the hills until it covers the land. Water is everywhere. The rain continues to come down in torrents, day after day.

Finally the rain stops. No more gloomy days, and no more puttering of the raindrops on the roof all day and all night. The next morning Noah opens the door and steps out on the deck and watches the waters shift the broken limbs in the surf below. Day by day the water recedes, until finally the boat bumps land and stops shifting in the tossing water. They all stand on deck and look around. Nothing looks familiar. They are on the other side of the storm, but now they are in a brand new world.

When Noah arrived in his new world he was deeply troubled. He and his family were safe but he wondered how many others might not have survived. One big question troubled his mind. How could a God of new beginning be so destructive? His world had been devastated. His friends were gone. How was he to understand what had happened? Surely this was not the way to way to think about God.

As Noah looked down at all the mud and debris surrounding the ark, he heard God speaking in a saddened voice. "I solemnly promise you and your children . . . that I will never again send another flood to destroy the earth. And I seal this promise with this sign; I have placed my rainbow in the clouds as a sign of my promise until the end of time, to you and all the earth." (Genesis 9:8-13 Selected verses)

Then Noah looked up the lingering clouds and saw a great rainbow stretching across the valley of his new world. As he marveled at that colorful arch in the sky, a new understanding of himself was emerging. He was the ark now. He was the carrier of the vision of a new tomorrow. The ark was only a bridge between what was past and what would be future. Storms come. But that's also when rainbows appear, arching over a land of new beginning."

Granddad paused, took a deep breath, and said. "It's a story. Just a story, but what a story!

It's a story about a new beginning beyond a tragic old ending. It's about a chance to start again and turn old yesterdays into a new tomorrows. It's just a story, but not too different from real life where the storms don't have to be "Noah size" in order for any of us to need to see rainbows and announce a new beginning. Finding something to blame for the disasters of yesterday is not nearly as important as finding a way to build a new success on top of failure. Each of us, in fact, the whole human family have places in the story where we can't change the past, but can build a new and wiser future. Not all failures are disasters, but they can be new starting places. We are the choosers. We can stand on top of our failures and use them as stepping stones. There is no Olympic athlete who has not fallen and had to get up and try again before being awarded a gold medal. All our floods will have their own dark nights and rainy days before we look up and discover rainbows arching in the sky as a big sign telling us to dream on. Gold medals are never hung around the neck of quitters. The national anthem is played for those who begin again and build new tomorrows.

A story is a word picture of an idea. We are story tellers. Whatever the size and scale of our floods, our rainbows need to be dream size, colored with advances in science, technology, and the guiding markers of Big Ten Universal Qualities.

Those who go on expeditions in search of Noah's old ark may at the same time miss out on finding the meaning of his story. It's not a story about wooden beams and pegs so much as about moving from a bad yesterday to a new tomorrow of hope and promise. It's about building bridges to a tomorrow worthy of our place in the story in the greatest time of history Noah's successors have ever known.

Even though we stand on the deck of a wonderful new age, the vision must be of yet newer and better tomorrows.

Yes, there are scoffers out there ready to make fun of our dreams. There are still some people who laugh at bridge build-ers, choosing rather to cling to old political, religious, and social platforms and ignore the amazing potential awaiting new builders of arks.

A sweeping look at the progression of the human family in the story of civilization will show that we have arrived in a new world – an age of unparalleled new enlightenment. It has taken a long time and lots of turbulent storms, but we are a part of the earth story in a brand new day.

A survey of our story up to now will indicates that the earth has been a stage-in-the-making for around four and a half billion years, before it became the setting for the earliest human family around six hundred thousand years ago. Across those early years, through religion and mythological stories, people tried to understand and explain what was happening.

When we fast-forward across the centuries, we note the rise of many early cultures, then Hebrew, Greek, Egyptian, and Roman civilizations, and successive new eras. Aristotle tried to put it all together in terms of what forces were causing things to be as they were. Copernicus began to sense that the earth was part of a larger system, with the sun and stars. Galileo advanced an earlier version of the telescope and observed that it was not the earth that was at the center of the solar system, but the sun. The spread of knowledge advanced rapidly when Gutenberg invented the printing press to make knowledge available to more people.

Now the Hubble Telescope circles the earth and is peering beyond – to distant galaxies. We now know we are only a tiny speck in the Milky Way galaxy, and that it is but one of billions of galaxies, reaching across billions of light years into an indefinable distance.

Our science and the tools of technology have launched today's Noah family into a new world of computers, microscopes, particle accelerators, and cameras. With the tools we have created, we are discovering the molecular nature of our existence and the DNA blueprint by which we are made. We peer into the future and know that we have only just begun to make new inquiry about the nature of existence, and our place in the cosmos. So, here we are, in a brand new world – the Noah family, standing on the deck and looking out at new tomorrows.

I have heard some of today's Noah's, speaking and telling about the rainbows they see. I hear them speaking on a platform that science and technology is building, looking up at the clouds of new insight and seeing rainbows that reach beyond yesterday to new tomorrows.

Many of the speakers who make presentations at the annual World Future Conferences are visionaries. Many writers are talking about their rainbows in magazines like Technology Review, Wired, The Futurist, Scientific American, Popular Science, even Time Magazine. Other magazines, and many books are expanding the vision of our future into descriptions of what may be just ahead. I have been among those who celebrate, with growing hope, this reach for a new tomorrow, as noted scientists, business persons, researchers, educators, and adventurers share their insights as rainbows of promise.

In the beginning of the twenty-first century, these modern day Noah explorers build scenarios which enable us to march ahead and explore new possibilities. There projections may be a vision in progress, but we listen with great interest as these Noah stories are shared that tell us about new tomorrows with rainbow possibilities!

They speak of a longer time we will have for a place in the story. Our future life expectancy may exceed our eighty years by as much as another forty years. They awaken our interest when they talk about having robots to clean our houses. They make us impatient as we wait for cars that drive themselves. Computers will analyze MRIs and ultrasound. We will be able to overcome genetically based diseases like cancer, Alzheimer's, diabetes, and multiple sclerosis. With new applications of biotechnology, nanotechnology, and regenerative medicine we will be able to build new hearts, lungs, and livers. Through genetic engineering we will be able to direct cell behaviors. We will be able to extend the capacity of our brains to enhance our intellectual capacity. Computers will handle information on a far larger scale than ever before. As the power of non-biological intelligence merges with our biological intelligence, we may be able to input vast amounts of information into the brain. Artificial intelligence will expand the boundaries of experience, equal to imagination and fantasy. Imagineers think of sending robots to the moon to dig into its surface and build a permanent human habitation, and from there, to launch into deep space. Visionaries continue to work on creating nuclear fusion, or capturing the energy of volcanoes. Visions include multiple nations collaborating together to achieve projects beyond the scope on any one nation.

These scenarios include those who believe that we can learn how to take care of our earth so that it will be a sustainable home for the human family a thousand years into new ages. Even if the future does not follow such visionary tracts completely, these leaders of tomorrow still represents Noah in a new world.

The story of one Noah entrepreneur continues to be a model for rainbows in our age of innovation. He is a scientist at the Massachusetts Institute of Technology who began to build a rainbow vision of One Laptop Per Child. Nicholas Negroponte did research, brought together financial resources, and launched his ark. It's a dream in progress, but already thousands of children in remote parts of the world now have laptop computers they proudly use at school and then take to their modest homes, where they continue to explore the world with a tool which lets them see a new world. In villages in the remote parts of Peru, children are given those little green and white computers. Teachers are learning how to use them, then teach children how to use them, who live in farm villages where they have never even seen a tractor. A farmer father proudly stands by watching his little boy explore the world on that little vehicle of connections, and proudly boasts that his son knows how to use it.

Nicholas Negroponte is representative of many who are creating crossover ways of enhancing human capacity aligned with computer power in the new world. The rainbows of caring, compassion, and collaboration are joining together in the building of arks of hope in our time when we have our greatest chance in all our human story to turn problems into opportunity.

I see rainbows. I know tools alone don't make rainbows. They never will. But when new tools are linked with humanity's best qualities, rainbows appear on new horizons. As we expand the tools of science, we must also make sure we define an infrastructure of overarching defining qualities to guide the ways we use the succession of new tools in our hands – rainbow qualities of **kindness** and **caring**, **honesty** and **respect**. When these qualities are the identity markers by which the people of the world family define who we are in successive new worlds, they help us to be people of **collaboration** and **tolerance**, **fairness** and **integrity**, built by **diplomacy** and **nobility**. These are not just qualities to measure by, but qualities to live up to. They form a rainbow call from the future. It's this rainbow of qualities that the children of the world need to learn, at the same time they are using little screens to link to new worlds.

These rainbow vision words which define civilization's best qualities, are not religious, or secular, just very important leading-edge, defining qualities anyone in our world family can choose, while embracing many associations and sub-identities, Buddhist, Christian, Moslem, religious, or non-religious. They simply define us as we can be when we reach for the next level up in our quest for our best life. These world-family overarching qualities can never be mandated. They are self-chosen identity markers.

I see rainbows. My mother helped me see rainbows, many years ago now. We sat here on this porch and I sat on her lap as a little four year old boy and listened as she read stories from a farm journal magazine, which introduced new ways to work the land, with new tools. That magazine included stories about a little black boy, like the one I played with while my mother visited a tenant family neighbor the next house down the dusty road. Those stories helped me see a bigger world. This old porch may be a deck on Noah's Ark from which we can see tomorrow and build rainbow vision.

In the old apocalypse story and paradigm, God was going to fix the world by starting over with a new family. But even then, the tomorrows of new hope and promise would not be up to God, but up to Noah and his family. God was saddened by his failure, but there on the deck stood Noah. It was for him and his descendant that God painted a rainbow of promise in the sky. They were the new ark between yesterday's dark past and tomorrow's bright future.

People are carriers of the rainbow visions. Storms still come — cyclones in Nyanmar, earthquakes in Haiti, Chili, Taiwan, Japan, tornadoes across many places in our country, floods on the great plains and coasts, hurricanes, oil spills in the Gulf, fires in the west — and personal storms which arise wherever people stand in the face of life on both their chosen and un-chosen journeys. That's where we stand. We are on deck now. Our name is Noah. It's here we can see rainbows.

In this new world, our understandings keep changing. Like Noah, our understanding of God is changing. We can no longer accept the view of God as being angry and vindictive, who destroys the earth and its family. Never again can we use the metaphor of God as a penalizing judge, exacting wrath and endless punishment. Instead, we are beginning to understand God as a part of our story. With our new paradigm of a molecular understanding of existence and our interaction with its forces, we see ourselves as those who are responsible partners with all the macro and micro forces of molecular existence. As designers of tomorrow, we are in need of a magnanimous rainbow vision which helps us to build our new world with great care and wisdom. We need more and better technology, but that is not enough. We need to reach for a humanity which is defined by our best human qualities.

In this new world we now understand that God is not a religious word. Inquiry about God can be pursued in the laboratory as readily as at church.

Our new adventures are sacred. Their altars of respect are everywhere. Noah's new world has never been so full of potential as it is now, when we are privileged to take our place in the progressive march of civilization. This is our time to see rainbows.

I watched the faithful devotion of two of my students who were parents of a new little baby boy whose beginning life was so very tenuous. He had a very rapid heartbeat. In their love and devotion, those anxious parents stayed at the hospital day and night so they could see rainbows and be bridge persons of hope for their little boy. They were Noah. With the help of other Noahs, the little boy lived and eventually went home to a life of good health. In this case, it was a team of Noahs – doctors, nurses, technicians, engineers, and builders of complex digital machines – all of these made the successful passage possible. Beyond that, it was no accident that there was a great hospital there, staffed and ready to be an ark with high tech equipment. Many people had been playing Noah, lots of them – in the community, schools and universities, in medical school and research laboratories – ready to believe in tomorrow and link science and human compassion in a new techno-humanization venture where rainbows can appear. These can so overarch our religions and cultures that they become the defining qualities which can guide us to our best tomorrows. It's the new sacred.

We are at a great start over point in history. The next fifty years will have a critical impact on the next five hundred years. The advancement of science and technology, combined with the Big Ten Universal Qualities, provide us unparalleled opportunity to embark on rainbow tomorrows.

How long does each of us have to look for rainbows? One lifetime. But that is enough. That's our immortality. We do not need to live forever to see rainbows and build bridges between yesterday and tomorrow – between what was and what can be.

All of you have been to our retirement house where your Grandmother and I live now. And you have been in my office and have seen my rock collection on the bookcase directly across from my desk. I call it a clock. It measures on a cosmic time scale. One rock is from the brush-covered desert area of Wyoming, where a million years earlier it had been in an ancient lakebed, before a break in the terrain let those snow-fed waters empty into the Pacific Ocean. So I picked up one of those stones and brought it home to be a part of my rock clock, where time is measured in millions of years, instead of hours or minutes. It's round and shows the layers of sediment which went into its formation year after year, storm after storm, before it hardened and then broke into pieces, and after that, rolled in water until it was shaped into a beautiful round ball. You have heard me tell you what it is, that is a dinosaur egg. That's when you look at me in disbelief, which says, 'Granddad, that's not true.' So I correct the story and tell you what it really is, that it's really Fred Flintstone's bowling ball. And you still didn't believe me.

One rock is petrified wood, representing a time when trees were a part of the landscape long ago – so long ago that it took on, and became one with, the elements around it. Another rock clock is volcanic rock. It's from Hawaii. And, no, the evil spirits didn't follow me home for taking it. In fact, I didn't take it. A teenager brought it back as a souvenir to give to me. That volcanic rock is the youngest one there. It's like only a minute of time compared to the age of other old rocks on that tray. If you compare the length of our entire life to any stone there, it is just barely one tiny tick on this clock of time. But in that one tick, we are now in the age of the new sacred where we can combine science and technology with our Big Ten Universal Qualities of **Kindness, Caring, Honesty, Respect, Collaboration, Tolerance, Fairness, Integrity, Diplomacy, Nobility.**

The time has come for us to build new arks. It's time to define who we are in the lengthening human story in terms of the ways we can help launch a new world of great hope and promise. In ways, unique to whatever storms we face, each of us can be a new Noah, and stand on deck in our new world and look for rainbows.

But for now, how about some free time – maybe a game of roller-bat, or softball, out in the barn yard, before we all make our way down to the meadow for a cookout before sunset? Who votes that that?"

CHAPTER THREE

Picking Up The Broken Pieces

'I have enough, my brother.'

GRANDDAD WAS EVEN MORE RELAXED THAN USUAL, AS HE SAT IN his plastic armchair and leaned back, with his legs crossed. Being down on the farm meadow was one of his favorite places. In his usual cordial manner, he said, "Steve, I want to thank you for helping to create this setting where we have now gathered down here on the grassy farm meadow, near the lake and beside the spring-fed branch which winds its way through this valley. I know you were drawing on your Boy Scout camping experience to lay the campfire, while I was putting the plastic arm chairs in a circle. I add my thanks to all of you who pitched in and helped your grandmother get all the things together for our wiener roast, including the drinks, and the fixings for the ever famous campfire s'mores. So, who wants to do the ceremonial lighting of the campfire?"

"I'll do it." Marsha volunteered immediately. "That is, if it's all right with Steve. He's the one who fixed it, so all the skill I need is just to strike a match to the right spot."

They sat around in the circle of chairs and watched the smoke curl in the air as the flames began to wind up through the wood. Now that the sun was setting, it was cool enough that, instead of just sitting in the circle of chairs, some got up from time to time to back up to the fire.

After all of them had shown their skills at roasting hotdogs on a stick and then roasting marshmallows for their s'mores, they sat around sipping Coke and Sprite and telling yarns about childhood days here on the farm when they came to visit.

Light from the campfire glowed as darkness closed in gradually and Granddad began the story everyone was waiting for.

"I wanted us to meet down here in the meadow," Granddad said. "I keep it mowed for just occasions such as this. Of course, when I was here as a boy, it was pasture land, so the cows kept it mowed for us. We always had one or two cows so we could have milk, cream, cottage cheese, and country butter. How many times have we gathered here to roast hotdogs like this? I have no count, but I always delight in having all of you and your parents down here for an evening campfire dinner, with lots of fun and talk. Sometimes it's late and the campfire has burned down to glowing coals before we douse the coals, turn and leave these delightful times together. But now, you honor me by waiting for me to tell another story. This one is about Jacob, and his twin brother, Esau, and a night Jacob spent, under the stars, probably wishing he had a campfire like this to be around with his family. But that was no longer possible, far from it. So, let me tell you a story I have en-titled, Picking Up The Broken Pieces. It's a story about identity, profiled in considerable contrast by two brothers and how they approached their desire for wealth.

It was almost dark, out there in strange new territory. Jacob looked around in the encroaching darkness for a place to lie down for the night after an exhausting day of frantic walking. He needed some way to elevate his head. There was no soft pillow like he usually had. He found a loose rock and pulled it around so he could put his head on the flatter side and lie down to sleep, tired and bewildered. He thought anxiously about his surroundings and wondered what dangers lurked in the darkness. The sun had set and there was no moonlight. Stars appeared and stared back at him in the darkness as he lay on his back and looked up with open eyes. His mind recalled the vivid scenes of the day he had just scrambled through.

The day had started uneventfully and it seemed nothing unusual when Esau came up to Jacob's tent, where he was boiling some lentil stew over an open fire.

'Jacob, give me some of your stew,' Esau demanded.

'All right,' Jacob said lightly. 'I'll be glad to share some, just as soon as you share with me.'

'What do you want?' Esau answered glibly.

'Just the birthright you hold to this place around here. You give me that and you can have the stew.'

'It's yours,' Esau said, as he reached for a clay bowl and held it out for Jacob to fill. 'It's not worth that much to me anyway, especially when one is as hungry as I am.'

It wasn't long before their father called from the adjacent tent. 'Esau!' Isaac called out. 'Esau, come over here.'

Esau gulped the last bit of stew, set his empty bowl down, and hurried over to his father's tent.

Esau's mother had heard his father call and wondered what her blind husband could want. So she followed Esau across the camp, but stopped outside the old brown tent to listen.

'Esau,' his father said, 'it's late in the morning and I'm hungry. Go out and find me something to eat. As soon as you do that, I will confer the birthright blessing on you, which is your right as my older son.'

Always ready for outdoor activity, Esau lifted the flap of the tent to leave, 'I'm on my way,' he said quickly.

Rebecca stepped to one side and hid at the corner of the tent. Esau did not see her as he headed for the open fields.

Hurriedly, Rebecca rushed back over to the tent where Jacob was finishing his own stew. 'Come inside,' Rebecca said. 'Jacob, you heard your father call to Isaac to come into his tent. Well, I was outside and overheard him talking. He asked Esau to bring him something to eat and then he would confer the birthright blessing on him. We both know what that means after your father dies. It means that Esau will inherit all he owns and you will get nothing. Tradition!' Disdain was in her voice, as she uttered it again. 'Tradition! The first born gets the inheritance. That's the tradition in this family, but it's not right. Not right at all. You two are twins and born only moments apart. You deserve the inheritance just as much as Esau. So here's what I want you to do, and do quickly. Go to my tent and get some stew I am preparing. Take it to Isaac just like it is Esau bringing in the food he requested. He's old, blind, and hungry. He'll never know the difference.'

'He'll know,' Jacob responded quickly. 'He'll know if he reaches out and touches me like he always does to know who's there. I don't have hairs on my arms like Esau.'

'Well, cover them up,' Rebecca said. 'I'll get you one of Esau's fur coats to wear.'

The sun was overhead and shinning brightly when Jacob stepped inside Isaac's dimly lighted tent with a bowl of stew on a tray.

'Back so soon?' Isaac questioned.

'It was easy picking today. Didn't have to go far.'

'Well, bring it here. I'm hungry,' Isaac said. 'I can't see you, so let me feel your arms.'

Nervously, Jacob placed the tray down in front of his father. Isaac reached out to feel who was there.

'Your voice sounds more like Jacob's voice. Are you sure you aren't fooling me?'

'My voice does sound a lot like his, sometimes. After all, we are twins. Here, touch my arms and you'll know.'

Isaac touched the fur on the coat sleeve briefly and then began feeling for the tray and the food.

'Prepared just the way you like it. A little touch of spice.' Jacob said. 'Enjoy it while I do a few other things. I'll be right back.'

Jacob stepped outside the tent where his mother was waiting. 'Did he confer the birthright on you?' she asked.

'Not yet,' Jacob said.

'Well, go back in and remind him of what he said,' Rebecca demanded. 'And, don't wait another moment. Esau may be back any time, now.'

Jacob lifted the tent flap and went back inside while Isaac was eating the stew. 'My kind father,' Jacob said softly, 'I am ready now for you to confer on me the blessing you promised earlier today, so we can keep up the tradition of our family.'

Jacob waited silently as Isaac said, 'Abraham, my father, fulfilled a great and honored tradition in his family of naming the first born son as the one to carry on as leader of the family. Now, it is my duty to name you as the one who is to carry that tradition forward. You are the one who must hand that tradition down to others. So I swear by my father and his father before him, you are now my heir.' Jacob thanked his father and promised to honor the tradition handed down from Abraham.

Rebecca had entered the tent quietly and stood listening. When Isaac had completed the blessing, she reached over and put her hand on Isaac's shoulder. She told Jacob he could leave, and she would bring out the tray.

It was just barely in time. She had just gotten back to her tent when she saw Esau coming to his father's tent, carrying in a big tray. Rebecca stood outside and listened.

'You have what?' came the thundering question in response when Esau said, 'I have the finest stew and bread you ever tasted, even some fresh wild berries.'

'More stew? You just brought me some. Are you Esau, or are you Jacob?'

'I'm Esau. Here, feel my arms and you can tell.'

Isaac didn't even reach out. 'I've been tricked by your brother,' he said. 'And I have conferred the birthright on the wrong son.'

'Well, just reverse it,' Esau said.

'I can't,' Isaac said. 'It's part of an oath given by my father, Abraham.'

'Well, then just confer part of it on me. That's all I need, or even want,' Esau said.

'I can't do that either,' Isaac said.

'Jacob's a deceitful thief,' Esau said. 'He has betrayed both of us. He has stolen the birthright from me. But I can take care of that. It will be mine again just as soon as I get rid of him. I'll kill him!' Esau said in bitter anger, as he turned and stormed out of the tent in a rage.

Rebecca heard it all. She slipped away and rushed over to Jacob's tent. 'Jacob,' she said frantically. 'He knows. They both know. Esau is furious and threatening to kill you. You must get away now. Quickly! I can't protect you against him if he comes in here. So leave now. Go to my brother's place in Haran. Here he comes. Leave! I will distract Esau long enough for you to get away.'

Quickly Jacob lifted up the back side of the tent and slipped under. He headed for the cover of the forest at its nearest point and then for the mountains beyond. He pushed his way through the bushes and trees, putting as much distance as he could between himself and his brother. At times he would stop briefly, look back and listen, to see if he was being followed.

Sunlight faded quickly in the mountain valleys. It was soon so dark that Jacob was mostly feeling his way through the trees. He knew he had no choice but to stop and wait for daylight before he continued to his Uncle Laban's place. He fumbled around in the darkness until he found a rock he could use for a pillow.

Jacob rested his head on the rock pillow. It was hard. Sleep waited and waited. Jacob lay there in the darkness, looking up through the trees at the stars, reliving the tangled events of the past few hours. The foolishness of what had happened so quickly crowded his mind. He had deceived his father and unleashed the fury of his brother, only to become a refugee from his home and family. He had never felt more lonely in his life. It was like he was at the end of the road.

When a restless sleep finally came, Jacob dreamed a strange dream. There was a stairway reaching from earth to heaven. Angels were going up and down on that stairway. There, at the top of the stairway, God was standing. God spoke to Jacob and reminded him of the inheritance he had stolen and also lost in the same day. But then God spoke of the inheritance which could not be lost – the unbreakable covenant he had made with his father, Isaac, and before that, with his grandfather, Abraham. There stood God, asking him to be the one to extend that link from the past into a long future and a great family.

Then Jacob woke up. Wide awake now, he reflected on the dream. It seemed like God had not given up on a run-away boy, that, instead of being at the end of the road, he was somehow at a strange new beginning. The dream was so vivid he could hardly believe he was on earth. But he was. In the stillness he talked to himself. "God lives here! I've stumbled into his home! This is the awesome entrance to heaven." (Genesis 28:16, 17)

He could see it now – how haughty, selfish, and heartless he had been in his dealings with his brother. But the strange dream made him feel like he could go on beyond the wrongs of the past and still claim a good future.'"

Granddad looked down briefly. When he looked back up, he said, "This story has its counterpart in all of us as we become Jacob on our chosen and un-chosen journeys, and pillows are hard, and we desperately need a new beginning beyond some old ending. We may not see a stairway to heaven, with angels going up and down on it, but we all have a call to be worthy of the heritage we have received and can extend into the future as our part in the earth family story.

The lengthening birthright of passing generations calls upon us to use what we are given as stewards of the endowment of the ages. It's a birthright multiplied now through science and technology, and rapid advances in knowledge. And when change invades, and when nights are long and pillows are hard, that is the most important time to let our highest identity extend beyond our failures and imperfections so we can be free to go forward."

The sun was already beaming down when Jacob woke up the next morning. The dream was still fresh in his mind, with a sense that God would help him find a new tomorrow beyond his failed yesterday. He pulled on the rock he had laid his head upon, and turned it up on the end as a kind of pillar of hope. In the silence he said to himself, 'The name of this place is Bethel – house of God.'

Now Jacob was the one who was hungry and would give most anything for some stew, but he simply had to press on toward his uncle's place. Jacob climbed up on a small hillside so he could see into the distance, then began to make his way across miles and miles of new territory.

When he finally arrived at Haran he came upon a gathering of shepherds at a well. They were waiting until all the shepherds got there before they began drawing water from the well for their sheep. When the last flock of sheep gathered, to Jacob's surprise, it was led by a girl. When it came time for her to water her sheep, Jacob rushed up to the well and began drawing water for her flock. She stood by and watched him perform his act of kindness. For Jacob, it had become more than an act of kindness. The emotions of love rushed his mind. The beauty of this young girl captivated his full attention. He wanted to know who she was.

'My name is Rachel. My father is Laban.' she replied in response to his question.

Jacob burst into an exclamation of full surprise. 'Your father and my mother are brother and sister!' he said. 'I am Jacob, Rebecca's son.'

'My father will be very glad to see you,' was Rachel's quick response, as she rushed up to give him a welcoming hug. It was a hug Jacob returned, and never forgot.

Laban welcomed his nephew and treated him like family. Jacob began to work with his uncle. As they worked together, everybody could tell that Jacob and Rachel were in love. It wasn't long before Jacob asked Laban if he and Rachel could be married.

Tradition! Tradition required that the older daughter be the first to marry. Laban tricked Jacob into marrying Rachel's sister, Leah. A week later Laban bargained with Jacob to work for him for seven years, then he could marry Rachel. They were so in love that the years went by quickly.

During that time Jacob did some trickery of his own. He bargained to have the sheep and goats with mixed color for his own, while all the solid color animals would belong to Laban. Jacob was the one who took care of the animals each day, and managed them so the new ones born would have mixed color and belong to him. As a result, Jacob became a wealthy man.

But beyond all his success was the silent pain of the conflict which had erupted in his family back home. Even while he was tricking his uncle, the memory of tricking his father haunted him. The recurring thought of somehow meeting his brother, who had vowed to kill him, awakened paralyzing fear. The fear was always there, causing him to look around constantly, thinking his angry brother might show up. As those haunting memories invaded his mind day after day, he decided that he just had to go back and face his past. He wanted to forget about the inheritance. He didn't even need it now. With a measure of pride he could tell Esau that he could have all of the inheritance.

Jacob planned a journey back home. He could take his servants and his growing family back with him and introduce his wives and children. And he could make a generous gift to his brother – lots of sheep, goats, cows, camels, and mules. But would his brother still be angry? Would he even speak to him? He had to find out. Jacob planned to meet him in such a way that his anger might be diminished.

As Jacob traveled with his family, herds, and servants, he sent a runner out to tell Esau that he was coming home. But the runner came back with the news that Esau was coming out to meet him with four hundred soldiers. Jacob felt immense fear. He knew his servants would be no match against even a small army. He could retreat but knew he could soon be overtaken. All he could do was go forward with his plan and face his brother.

In an attempt to assuage whatever anger Esau felt, Jacob sent gifts to his brother in waves. First he sent a flock of sheep. Then he sent a herd of goats. Then other animals, all as a kind of gift to appease Esau's anger. Then finally, Jacob followed the last gift. He could see Esau in the distance. Jacob walked ahead many steps, then bowed to the ground. He walked ahead again and then bowed again, until he had bowed seven times. They were now very close together, but Esau had not called on his soldiers to attack. Instead, Esau walked out, all by himself, to meet his brother. He extended his open arms in a gesture of welcome. Jacob was immensely relieved and rushed up to meet his brother.

As soon as the embrace ended, Esau asked Jacob what was the meaning of all the flocks and herds he had just met.

'They are gifts,' Jacob said proudly. 'I want you to have them.'

Esau responded with laughter. 'I have enough, my brother. Keep what you have.'

'Is our father still alive?' Jacob asked immediately.

'He is,' Esau said.

'I must see him.' Jacob said. 'Do you think he will receive me?'

'Receive you? Indeed he will!' Esau responded emphatically. 'The heartbreak of many years will be healed.'

As the story is extended in the Bible, Jacob is the one who represents the link in extending the family story on down through his son Joseph, then Moses, then David and Solomon. But it's Esau who represents a role model for a very important identity. Esau is the one who turned loose of a broken past, to build a new future. He represents the best in human relationships, where one forgives yesterday so he can celebrate a new tomorrow. He is the one who was confident enough about life to say, "I have enough, my brother."

If we look back on that old journey story enough to sort out blame, it first lies with an unfair system that rewards tradition so much that it cripples newness.

Next, the fault lies with Rebecca, Jacob and Esau's mother, who played favorites and tried to right the wrong with deception, and a new wrong.

Beyond that comes Laban's deception of his nephew, who tricked him into marrying his older daughter, Leah, instead Rachel, the one he loved.

In turn, Jacob tricked Laban to gain an unfair part of his wealth. But it was a wealth that did not heal old hurts, or the brokenness of self respect and betrayal. What brought healing was Esau's refusal to hold on to the past at the expense of the future. He had made his wealth on his own, without waiting for an inheritance to come his way. Out of that self-reliant living, he did not need to be bought off by Jacob's attempt to impress him with his bribery gifts. He could say, 'I have enough, my brother.'

Esau is the real hero in the story and the one who models our own need to make honorable human relationships the leading identity marker that creates new tomorrows beyond old yesterdays. That person is the hero who picks up the broken pieces and put together a new future. The identity story ends years later, with

Jacob and Esau going together to carry their deceased father to his burial place.

The story, from beginning to end, is about identity. It's about choosing who we are, and who we want to be, on both our chosen and unchosen journeys, a taker or a giver. In our time in history, the resource base out of which we decide what we want to become and what will give to life, is immensely large, and getting larger every day in our age of growing knowledge, science, and incredible technological development. We get to decide if we will be one who adds respect and integrity to the amazing progression of human potential. Out of life's immense resource base, the future we ask for becomes our request of life. We have a place in the ongoing heritage that is passed on to new generations."

The glow of the campfire had grown dim. The surrounding darkness invited silence. Finally Granddad said, "As I look into the glimmering coals of the campfire, I reflect on my journey story. The twins of greed and generosity have both been within, and I may never have been completely one or the other. Between Jacob's grasp for the birthright, and Esau's 'I have enough,' I wonder how much I have been like Jacob, and how much I have been like Esau. What I hope is, that I have been enough like Esau so I can say, 'I have enough,' so I can pick up the broken pieces along life's chosen and unchosen journeys and keep putting the promise of the future ahead of the brokenness of the past. The big, overarching question is not, how much can I get, but how much can I give."

CHAPTER FOUR

Should Joseph Forget His Dreams?

We can put the past behind us and the future before us
in such a way that, as we meet challenge, we also meet opportunity.

SUMMERTIME WAS IN FULL SWING. SHORT-SLEEVE FREEDOM WAS A continuing invitation to be out at the farm. The green of towering oaks and flowing bamboo framed the white, two-story, house in the country where Granddad had grown up. He came out here often on weekends to think, write, and share time with his family. On this special day, he would be privileged to tell more stories to his young adult grandchildren. He was already out on the porch and sitting in his chair, reading some notes, when Grandmother came from the kitchen and placed her tray of cookies and pitcher of tea on a little table, followed by her grandchildren. Granddad waited for all of them to reach for another cookie and find a chair, then reached over and picked up a couple of cookies for himself.

"Let me begin today by telling you once again what a privilege all of you are giving me by letting me tell some of my stories. I have told them as launch-pad metaphors in my classes at the university, and am putting them together in a new book. But, it's telling them here that is of immense pride for me." He filled his tea glass from the pitcher Grandmother had placed on the table, took a sip of tea, and leaned back a little more in his chair. "As I tell these stories, I continue to insert some of my philosophy of success and self-development, which always points to the responsibility we have for our own success. The story I begin with today is about a special kind of success, that can be achieved in spite of many obstacles. It shows how we can turn tough journey into touchstone journey.

My story begins with a question, 'Who said Joseph should forget his dreams?'

The story of Joseph is so basic and recurring in life experience that the story could have happened anywhere, and anytime. But it happened in Palestine and Egypt, long ago, when times were very different. That difference doesn't matter all that much, because good stories give crossover insights by contrast and comparisons, as they outlive their time and become timeless metaphors and carriers of paradigms. They become mirrors to help us see ourselves.

As I retell Joseph's story, I seek to honor the storyteller of old, who mixed imagination and history. I want to mix imagination and metaphors, and create recurring little philosophical inserts that I call, *The Joseph Dream Vision*. So, it's not just Joseph's story, it's the story of all who dare to keep reaching for success beyond disappointment and struggle, by giving the best they have in the worst of times.

A grove of old olive trees surrounded the cluster of tents where Jacob lived with his shepherd family. Small trees and bushes grew near the spring at the oasis. The desert winds rustled the flaps of the tent as Jacob and his family gathered one morning for breakfast. Joseph was next to the youngest of Jacob's sons, and the one who bounced in, plopped down on the carpet, and began telling a dream he had just dreamed. 'We were all out in the field binding wheat into bundles. It was so funny, the sheaf that represented me was just standing there, and the sheaves, which represented you, were bending over and bowing to my sheaf. I am not sure I can explain it.'

'I don't have any trouble explaining it,' one of his brothers countered in sarcasm. 'You think you are better, and that you are going to be more successful than any of the rest of us. Well, we'll just see about that. As soon as you get a little older, we'll see how well you can round up stray sheep. So, if you are the best at herding stubborn, unpredictable sheep back to the fold, then we just might let you join us, provided of course, you don't expect us to bow down to you.' The other brothers burst out into boisterous laughter. 'Meanwhile, pull off that silly multicolored coat and eat your breakfast. Forget your stupid dreams.'

It was a rough beginning, but Joseph dared to tell another dream. This time he told about the moon and stars bowing down to him. It wasn't the particulars of Joseph's dreams that were significant, but that Joseph believed his dreams were foreshadows of the future."

The Joseph Dream Vision. We know, now, that sleep dreams are mostly jumbled images and mysteries, not to be taken seriously. But we also know that the awake dreams that children and young people entertain about the future, are important early indicators of identity and who they see themselves becoming. These vision images preset the mind and program how the brain assimilates and uses information to interpret life. In fact, those identity dreams program life in such a way that they become a talisman, an alter ego, a kind of relentless vision leader, day after day, year after year, even if those vision-dreams seem to get abruptly displaced by adversity or hardship.

Some of our dreams are self-image projections of who we would like to be. Dreams run scenarios in our own story. They are picture-thinking. We need to be sure we are painting a picture of the best we can be. For that to happen we have to think right, then make wise choices.

There are people who can help us think right. We can seek them out. There are books which can help us think right. We can find them, read and re-read them. These can help us set high expectations. Beyond these, the most important guidance does not come from without, so much as from within. We can tell ourselves who we want to be and our mind will become our own guiding dream-maker — our Identity GPS.

It's important to dream our best dreams.

"Surprise and mystery were beginning to play out in Joseph's life. Joseph was surprised, but immensely pleased, with a coat of many colors his father gave him. Talk about being proud of a coat, Joseph's esteem soared every time he put on that distinctive coat. Of course, his brothers didn't think much of his coat, and that may be part of the reason they scowled at him when he told his dream stories. But Joseph kept wearing that coat until it was getting too small for his youthful growing body.

They were shepherd people, and Jacob's older sons often led the sheep to distant grazing lands in search of grass. It meant they were sometimes gone for many days. One day Jacob began wondering where his sons were and decided to send Joseph to search for them.

It was a big day for Joseph. Not only did he feel trusted by his father, but he might be included as a shepherd, like his brothers. So, with eager step, he set out from the grove of trees surrounding the tents, on a journey to find his brothers and the flock of sheep. Wearing that coat of many colors his father had given him seemed to honor the new mission he was privileged to carry out for his father. He imagined the special welcome he would receive by his older brothers.

Many miles later, he climbed up on a steep, rocky hillside,

shaded his eyes with his hand, and searched. When he spotted his brothers, still far away, he climbed back down and increased his pace, filled with excitement to be on a mission for his father, and ready to belong among the big brothers. As he made his way along the dusty trails, he had visions of their being so glad to see him they would come out to meet him. He approached the camp with hurried steps, and called out an exciting 'helloooo' from a distance. But no one was coming out to meet him. As he neared the tent, he slowed his pace to a halting walk. Finally he approached their glaring silence. 'What's wrong?' Joseph asked.

'What's wrong?' one of his brothers derided. 'Guess you wouldn't know, would you, wearing a fancy coat like that out here? Maybe you want to become the chief shepherd and let us bow down to you. Is that it, dreamer boy? Maybe you'd like to show us how. Go ahead. Bow down. Show us how.'

Joseph was only inching his way forward now, thinking they might come out and force him to his knees. They did approach, but instead of making him bow down, one of them yanked off his precious coat from behind. After holding Joseph's coat up and dangling it in the air as an object of derision, his brother dropped it on the ground. Joseph reached down to get it, but his brother quickly put his foot on it and twisted it in the dirt.

Other brothers approached and two of them grabbed Joseph's arms and began forcing him away from the camp. Soon Joseph saw they were approaching a dry well, and had no doubt now what they were planning to do. He began to resist with all his might, but to no avail. Even as he pleaded, 'Please, don't throw me in there,' they gave one final push and he went over the edge, bumping and scraping his way down to a stunning thud at the bottom of the pit. Slowly, Joseph pulled himself up and leaned back against the dirt walls of the pit. He was still alive. He looked up at the small circle of light above him. It was a shocking moment. This was not the way he had dreamed. It was everything but that. He had thought he would be looked up to by his brothers. Now he knew how much they hated him and looked down on him. How could he have been so naive? So gullible? It hurt to fall into the pit, but it hurt even more to be so rudely rejected by his own brothers. He wondered if they would leave him there to die.

How could he have been so foolish to believe in his dreams? Hadn't what just happened made a mockery of his dreams? Now he wondered if he would ever get out of the pit. But he had taken the dreams so seriously. He thought they were signals from the future. As he leaned up against the dirt walls of the pit, it seemed like it was time to forget his dreams. That's when new thoughts flashed in his mind, *maybe this is the time I need most to remember them, in spite of how impossible it seems.* Almost as part of his dream extended, he found himself repeating, *'I won't give up now. I will keep believing in possibilities. I won't give up now. I won't give up now!'* As he repeated the words, he found himself feeling the energy of hope – that, instead of feeling like he was at the end of the road, he was at a strange new beginning, in spite of how impossible it seemed now.

> ***The Joseph Dream Vision****. Sooner or later, most of us get thrown into a pit where the hard places we face in life can be, both an ending and a beginning. Instead of giving up, that is the time our dream visions can be affirmed as positive expectations. They don't prove anything, but they reset the emotions. We dare not give up on our dreams. The pit may be one of our best turning-point challenges.*
> **There's life beyond the pits***.*

Joseph's brothers turned their backs to the well and slowly made their way back to the tents and sat down. It was quiet. The shuffling movement and bleating of the sheep were the only sounds to be heard. Nobody said anything for a long while. Out of the stillness, Reuben turned his head to one side. 'Listen,' he said. 'What's that?' They all listened and then Reuben got up and walked in the direction of the sound. Now it was clearer. Amid a cloud of dust in the distance, he could see a line of camels, inching along the edge of a rocky hillside. 'Come and look,' he said. His brothers rushed over. The jingling sound of a bell gradually became louder.

'It's a caravan of traders,' one of the brothers said. 'Let's go out and meet them and see what they have to sell.'

'Better still,' Reuben said, 'Let's sell them something.'

'We don't have anything to sell that they would want, unless they want a sheep,' came the immediate reply.

'Who says we don't have anything to sell? I know one thing we could sell, and they would pay a good price for it,' Reuben countered.

'What's that?' one brother quizzed quickly.

'A slave. A boy slave. Joseph. They'll pay us good money for him.'

'Well, lets find out,' Judah said quickly. 'Let's pull him up and take him to them.'

'Not so fast,' Reuben said. 'Let's talk to them first. We can tell them we have something valuable they would like to see.'

When the traders arrived at the edge of the pit, they were eager to see what the shepherds had to offer. When a rope was thrown down to Joseph, he gladly took hold of it and began climbing out of the pit, thinking that maybe his dream was not really ending after all, just taking a new beginning. Once Joseph was out of the pit, and saw the traders, he knew what was happening; he was being sold by his own brothers. He watched in helpless disbelief as his brothers accepted twenty pieces of silver for him.

Joseph offered no resistance as the traders tied his wrists to-gether with a rope and then tied the other end to a pack on one of the camels. Resistance was not an option unless he wanted to be dragged through the desert. As he trudged along, he looked back and saw his brothers watching from the fading distance. He lifted his tied hands and waved to them as best he could. They didn't wave back.

A touchstone journey had begun.

The Joseph Dream Vision. *There are some experiences in life which are so defining, they become touchstone events.*

In early days of gold prospecting, there was a rock called a touchstone. Gold miners would take samples of their gold nuggets to town and find an assayer. When the assayer would rub the gold sample across the black, flint-like, touchstone rock, he could tell rather accurately by the mark left on the rock just how pure the gold was.

All of us get rubbed against touchstones, which reveal our true quality. We get thrown into the pit. So the question is, 'What will we do with that defining experience? Will we carry it with us across the years like a wound that we never let heal? Will we wear it like a badge of pity to show how we have been wronged and why we should therefore be exempt from real achievement? Or, instead of crying in self pity, will we see it as a pivotal moment for defining ourselves as a person with positive expectancy beyond hurt, loss, injustice, and struggle? Will we let the pit define us, or will we define the pit?'

Some of life's struggles are too small even to get our attention. But some are big enough and tough enough to be defining signals. Those may be the 'pit' for us, with potential to be touchstones. Often those experiences help build qualities, that become steps up to levels of success which never would have been possible without those qualities developed in the struggle. We can put the past behind us and the future before us in such a way that, as we meet challenge, we also meet opportunity. All the qualities and skills we develop in our pits can be the ones which help us maximize our potential beyond the pit.

Our pits can be touchstone opportunity to reveal our pure gold.

Darkness was approaching, so the Ishmaelite traders stopped and pitched camp for the night. To the surprise of the traders, Joseph offered to help with the work. Finally, after much persistence, one of the traders untied one of Joseph's hands and gave him some work to do in preparing food. Joseph was hungry and when dinner was ready, he ate with vigor. After dinner, a trader offered Joseph an old coat to keep him warm in the cold night desert air. He accepted it and pulled it on. Then his wrists were tied together again and the end of the rope fastened securely to a tent stake.

Sleep was long in coming. Joseph had to fight back the tears when he thought about how brokenhearted his father would be when he realized that his son, with his special coat of many colors, would not be coming back home.

Joseph learned that the traders were headed for Egypt. As a little boy, he had heard his great grandfather, Abraham, tell about seeing the great pyramids, and he wished he could see them some day. Now, as a strange coincidence, he might have that special opportunity. As he imagined the future, he began to feel the confidence of hope, and drifted into sleep.

The next morning Joseph helped with taking down the tent and packing the camels for the day's journey. He was eager to begin. New possibilities lay ahead.

The Joseph Dream Vision. Focusing on the promise of the future instead of dwelling on the regrets of an unchangeable past, is one of the mind's most creative powers. Even if it's largely imagination, that releases our best ideas and energy, and can be a focus on positive expectations. We can't change the past, but we can make it a part of our reach for a better future.

We can focus on the promise of the future, instead of dwelling on regrets from the past.

By the time the caravan got to Egypt the traders had begun to trust Joseph. He felt like one of the team as he helped set up the trading booths along the edge of the street to display their goods for sale. Just as they were beginning to greet their first customers, the leader of the caravan came over and handed Joseph a coat. It was just like the coats the other traders were wearing. Joseph put it on with a new feeling of pride. He was one of the team now. Up and down the street, other booths lined the market. When he looked far down the street, he could see the peaks of the pyramids in the distance. Joseph wished his brothers could see him now!

Four days later, two traders came to Joseph and said, 'Come with us.' Joseph didn't ask where they were going. He eagerly joined his fellow traders as they made their way through the city, past buildings more spectacular than any he had ever seen, and closer and closer to the great pyramids. More than ever, he wished his brothers could see him now!

When they came to a place where a lot of people were standing around, Joseph followed the traders through the crowd to where there was a raised platform. Both traders clinched Joseph's arms and led him over to where a man was seated at a table. One of them spoke to the man at the table and then turned to Joseph. 'Pull off your coat and strip to the waist, then get up on that platform.' Anxiously, Joseph looked at the crowd of men surrounding him. Trying to escape didn't seem like an option. Slowly, he did as he was told, with no doubt as to what was happening. He was being sold again.

Joseph's excitement about being in a new country and his pride in being a part of the trading team vanished. One of the traders took his coat, folded it across his arm, and stood and watched. Egyptian buyers gathered around. They asked him to turn around so they could see him better, then felt of his muscles.

The lead trader who had asked Joseph to come with him walked over to a man he seemed to have known already. He leaned over and said, 'Potiphar, you ought to bid on that young man.

Don't just look at his muscles; he has qualities you can't see. His brothers sold him to us up in Canaan, and he has traveled with us and worked with us for several days. He has become a good member of our team. If he's hurt and angry with his brothers, you can't tell it. He has never displaced it on us. Not once has he complained or seethed in bitterness and anger.'

The traders had never been told about Joseph's coat of many colors, or the esteem he felt when his father had given it to him. They didn't have to be told about his qualities. They could see those in all he did. The trader made one last comment to Potiphar before he stepped over and joined the circle of buyers. 'He's a cut above,' the trader said. 'He has class, real class. That's worth more than his good looks or strong body.'

> **The Joseph Dream Vision.** *Who would we have been, if we had been up there on the auction block? Would we have looked angry, and scowled at the buyers? Would we have hung our heads in embarrassment, self-pity, and defeat, hoping nobody would bid on such an unpromising person?*
>
> *Or, would we have been selling ourselves at our best, shoulders back, chin up, eyes alert, smiling, and exuding confidence, so the very best buyer out there would bid high, and be the one to place the final bid?*
>
> *The future is what we make it by the way we respond to the ever-changing present — to how we present ourselves every day, and especially in our critical defining moments.*
>
> **In our toughest moments, it's time, not merely to be sold, but sell ourselves at our best.**

As Joseph stood on the auction block, he watched the buyers as they decided if they would bid on him, and how much. He heard their bids, one after another. It was no time to look back in bitterness at how his own brothers had been responsible for what was happening. Now was not a time to think of the heartless way his brothers thrust him into the pit – no time to recall the painful sense of betrayal he felt when they sold him to strangers. It was not a time to cry in self pity, even though he was being betrayed again, and being sold at auction to the highest bidder, as just one more commodity, one more victim of injustice. In spite of all the wrongs, this was not the time to rehearse the past – it was a time to dream a new dream for a new future.

> ***The Joseph Dream Vision.*** *We know that so much of life's stage is set for us by others and by circumstance. We don't get to choose. Our best option is to play our part the best we can on life's un-chosen stages. That way, we are never merely sold – we are selling ourselves. By refusing to be only what the world makes of us, we dare to be what we make of ourselves, in spite of adversity, injustice, and hardship. We make the best of the worst, when we announce our freedom from life's most destructive masters – regret, anger, fear, hate, bitterness, greed, jealousy, resentment, and self-pity.*
>
> *We can take a, so what, approach, and dare to see our struggles as some kind of opportunity in disguise. We can note how many successful people have had their parallel to pits and auction-block moments, when hardship, struggle and injustice forced them to adjust to new reality. Like them, we can take our own, so what, approach. So what, we grew up as immigrants, or sharecroppers, or in the slums, or with handicaps, or other children made fun of our clothes, or the way we talked, we can use all that as extra incentive to work hard and learn forward. We dare not let the littleness of other people be an excuse to be little too. We can refuse to give up on our dreams of success, in spite of hardship, hate, and injustice. Day after day, year after year, we can make life into a school of enrichment*

instead of a ghetto of impoverishment. We can refuse to turn our struggle into an excuse to cry the disadvantage song, when, in fact, it could be the most important hurdles we ever jumped over and pushed on beyond. Like other people, who survive and transcend the pits, we can make the best of the worst. We can still do the best we can with what we have, never knowing what we have until we keep on trying.

With our own, so what, approach, we can adjust, compensate, reset the mind, and add extra incentive to put the past behind us and the future before us. We can sell ourselves at our best when it looks least like there are any buyers of importance around. We all arrive on a stage that is already set, no matter when or where we take our place in the human story. Even in our worst moments, when it seems no one is watching, we are passing our biggest auction-block test.

Build achievement on all of life's stages, great or small.

As Joseph stood there listening to the bids being announced, he began to hear a recurring bid from the person the trader had talked to earlier. Suddenly it became quiet. Then he heard the auctioneer announce, 'Sold.' Potiphar, a member of Pharaoh's personal staff, had placed the final bid. Joseph stepped down off the platform. Two of Potiphar's servants came up and led him away, still stripped to the waist.

It was an intense defining moment as Joseph was being led away. He had heard about slaves; now he was one. Instead of his dreams coming together, they seemed to be falling apart. Could he trade his coat of an Ishmaelite trader, for the coat of a slave and still fulfill his dreams?

As they all traveled along, Potiphar listened as Joseph responded to questions. In spite of having just been sold and bought as slave, he was positive. Potiphar began to realize what he wanted his new slave to do. With that kind of positive attitude and cordiality, he would have Joseph stand at the door and greet important foreign guests when they arrived. To Joseph's surprise, when he arrived at Potiphar's grand house, he was given the distinctive coat of a greeter.

If anyone had thought that it didn't matter how Joseph did his new job as a greeter, that no one would be paying attention, he would have been wrong. Joseph approached his new task with the same sense of pride he had exhibited when he was part of the trading team. It wasn't just a job, it was an expression of himself, and his persistent reach beyond regret for new opportunity. The quality of his workmanship was noticed by his fellow workers and his new owner. It wasn't long before he was promoted, and then promoted again, until he was advanced to being the administrator of Potiphar's entire household operations.

> **The Joseph Dream Vision.** *The principle of maximizing each opportunity, however small, is never played out on an isolated stage as though it were unimportant. It's a recurring dynamic for a successful life, that the person who has very little opportunity, but dares to take advantage of what little opportunity there is, that becomes the platform from which he makes even small steps to the next level up. The qualities manifested in life's hardest moments, reveal themselves again and again as increased insight, expanded mental and emotional power, and a larger outlook on life. The brain reprograms and develops new powers. Skills are awakened from their cocoon existence, which never would have come into play without the challenges big enough to awaken and release them.*
>
> *When life's auction blocks land us at Potiphar's house, it can seem like, one more tragedy, and be used as an excuse to be a failure. Or, on the other hand, it can be seen*

as a chance to win against great challenge, and to excel as one of life's zestful personalities, just in a new, unique setting. If we want to rank ourselves as successful people in spite of our tough situations, we dare not put life on hold, and wait for dramatic rescues, before we manifest our best. In the valley of struggle, we can climb up the hills of difficulty, step by step, in the relentless pursuit of respect and honor. It's no escape hatch or quick fix, and bad things can, and still do, happen, but in the meantime, we will be living with the creative energy of positive expectancy, which helps us turn crisis into birth and old endings into new beginnings.

Maximize your struggle opportunities.

The handsome young slave that Potiphar had secured from the auction block, now lived in a world of luxury and prestige. As a person of entertaining courtesy and distinctive cordiality, Joseph attracted the attention of Potiphar's wife. She liked him. Beyond that, she wanted him to sleep with her. Day after day she said flattering things which let her desires be known. Of course, Joseph noticed. It was a tempting offer. Could he get by with it? Human nature was pressing desire onto the stage.

It was not easy for Joseph to resist the interests of Potiphar's wife. One evening when he resisted her seductive interests, she embraced him and pulled him close. Joseph pulled away. She grabbed his coat and held on. But Joseph slipped out of the coat and quickly retreated to his quarters.

Potiphar's wife was insulted to have a servant rebuff and refuse her interest. She was humiliated and angry. She set out to get revenge. She went directly to Potiphar, holding Joseph's coat out in front of her, saying that his trusted servant had left his coat when he attempted to rape her.

Potiphar made an immediate response. He not only believed his wife's story, but had Joseph arrested and put in prison. The big wooden prison door slammed shut behind Joseph. Stillness invaded the cell. It was dark. The only light came from a small window in the door through which food was passed to prisoners. The light from that hole was even smaller than the circle of light at the top of the pit into which his brothers had thrown him. He was back.

Surely Joseph would forget his dreams now. Was this not the third great inhumanity he had suffered? First, the pit into which his brothers had pushed him, with the hurt of rejection. Then, being sold and deported to Egypt, and sold again on an auction block. And now this, blackmailed by a woman's injured pride and thrown into prison by her husband who believed her lies. Wasn't it time for Joseph to give up on his dreams and cry about how wrongly he had been treated at every turn, just when he needed to be climbing straight up the ladder of success, one more streak of bad luck after another? Hadn't the fall back made mockery of his dreams forever?

Just before the door of the prison had gone shut, the prison guard thrust an old coat into his hands and said, 'Here. You'll be glad to have this in there.' He was. It was cold and dark, damp and smelly. The coat was old and worn, but Joseph pulled it on. He went over and sat down on a wooden platform which he knew would be his bed. Surely this was the worst plight he had ever known.

> **The Joseph Dream Vision**. *When the worst comes, that is when it is most important to be our best. When the future looks darkest, that is the time to look beyond the blackness and see the glimmers of the light that hope can create.*
>
> *The Joseph dream vision is that we can renew our resolve and keep on trying in impossible situations. It is turning loose of the past so we can take hold of the future. It is looking up when wrong is pushing us down. It is seeking a new chance, instead of bemoaning an old loss. It is refusing to add up the wrongs which keep landing us on*

the penalizing side of injustice. It is looking for the good in the bad. It is being big when others are little. It is about doing right when others have done wrong. It is faith in tomorrow, instead of regret over yesterday.

To take hold of tomorrow, turn loose of yesterday.

In jail! Shock. Disbelief. Off with the coat of an administrator, and on with the coat of a prisoner. It was the pit again. It was the grossest of injustice. While he had been trying to make the right decision, he was being penalized and with little or no recourse. Was a great future now beyond reach? Hopeless? Many questions condensed into one big question, 'Was the dream over? Should Joseph forget his dreams?'

It would be easy for Joseph to build a prison within a prison, a prison in his mind by thinking depressive thoughts, to feel fear, anger, resentment, bitterness, and to respond in hostility. How could he avoid that double prison – the walls around him and the walls within his own mind? How could he reach beyond those limiting boundaries and put something better in their place? How could he dare to dream, when it seemed like the impossible dream?

If you expect to find Joseph lying over in the corner of his jail cell, broken, bitter, dispirited, refusing to eat or do anything for himself, you would be wrong. Instead, it was time to do something to make the best of the worst and the most of the least. He needed somewhere to begin. Thoughts, even little ones, could lead the way. Joseph saw that little window in the door as his window of opportunity. He went over to that little window and began saying something nice to the person who finally brought him something to eat. 'Hello,' Joseph said with courtesy. 'Thank you for bringing me some food. I appreciate your caring and kindness.'

It wasn't long before Joseph had become friends with the prison keepers and was drawn up from the prison cell and given work to do. Later he won favor with the prison master and was put in charge of other prisoners. He became their trusted friend. One prisoner, whom he befriended, by interpreting one of his dreams, was released from prison and found himself in a position to put in a good word for Joseph. He recommended Joseph as someone who could interpret a puzzling dream Pharaoh had dreamed. So Pharaoh asked for Joseph to be brought to him.

> **The Joseph Dream Vision.** *Building trusted and honorable networks of friendship and kindness among people, at any and all levels, is always some kind of opportunity. Nobody is too small or insignificant. Nobody is too big or important. Kindness is the key. And when people are not nice to us, it's not their test, it's ours — it's our opportunity to show how big we can be. When life is easy, it's no prize to win. The winning trophy can be a trophy for the triumph of honor when we are big toward others who are little toward us. We are winners when we go beyond the easy.*
> **Build good relationships everywhere.**

Once again, it was a change of coats for Joseph. Off with the jail coat and on with a coat in keeping with a visit to Pharaoh.

'You're going to do what?' a fellow prisoner exclaimed in surprise and disbelief, as he watched Joseph getting dressed in new clothes.

'I am going to visit with Pharaoh,' Joseph announced with enthusiasm, as he put on his new coat with pride and special care.

Pharaoh welcomed Joseph and moved quickly into telling his dreams. He said, 'I have learned that you can interpret dreams and I want you to interpret two strange dreams.'

The friend of prisoners was ready to be a friend to Pharaoh and listened carefully as Pharaoh told his dreams. Long days in prison, with no bread to eat because of grain shortage in Egypt, helped Joseph know the interpretation immediately. But did he dare give the right interpretation to Pharaoh? It would not be complimentary. If he told what he believed was the meaning of the dream, Pharaoh could be defensive and angry and send him right back to prison faster than he had left. It would be easy for Joseph to make up an interpretation that would flatter Pharaoh. Instead, at the risk of arousing Pharaoh's disfavor, Joseph proceeded to interpret the dreams truthfully.

> **The Joseph Dream Vision.** *Integrity is a matter of being honest with information and how we use it. Can we take our place in the human story as a person who can be trusted, whose name is as good as his word? Is that easy? No. But it can happen when we keep putting honor above personal gain in business, in sports, in family life, in intellectual pursuits. The opportunities keep recurring when we demonstrate that we can trusted to do the right thing.*
> **Honesty is one of life's highest qualities.**

Pharaoh had dreamed about fat cows being eaten by skinny ones, and about fat ears of corn being consumed by withered ones.

There was no magic in Joseph's interpretation of Pharaoh's dreams. Pharaoh had never lacked for plenty of the best food, but not so for prisoners. They had gone hungry many days because there was no bread. And there was no bread because there was no grain. Quietly, Joseph said, 'Your dreams mean that Egypt needs a grain reserves program in which some of the grain produced in the years of plenty is stored. Then that surplus can be drawn upon when there is an extended drought in the Nile valley and very little grain can be harvested.'

Joseph waited for a response. Pharaoh had listened carefully to the interpretation. Pleased with that practical insight, Pharaoh said. 'I understand my dreams now. It's true. We do need a grain reserve. And the person who understands the problem is the one I need to create that reserves program. You are not to return to prison, but come to the palace and set up such a reserves program and administer it.'

Instead of returning to prison, Joseph moved to the palace and was given rank and authority in Egypt, second only to Pharaoh himself.

> **The Joseph Dream Vision.** *No one knows how the future will unfold. Out of the unknown may come a serendipitous surprise. But even if not, it is no surprise that when we give our best to life, it becomes our best request of life. We set the signals which open the doorway for good things to happen. It may not always be that way, and tragic things happen to people who have given their very best into life. There are no guarantees. But while we are giving our best, we live with the positive emotions of hope, so that doorways open which would not have been there had we not kept on reaching out to give our best.*
>
> **Give your best to life, as your request of life.**

Joseph became an important part of Pharaoh's cabinet and a distinguished leader in Egypt. He was given a new coat to wear, which signaled his power and authority.

By now Joseph had worn seven coats. First, the coat of many colors which his father had given him. Second, the coat one of the traders had given him to fend against the cold desert air. Third, the coat of an Ishmaelite trader in the Egyptian marketplace. Fourth, the coat of a servant in Potiphar's house. Fifth, the coat of a prisoner in a cold, dark prison. Sixth, the coat of a person invited to interpret a dream for Pharaoh. And now, seventh, the coat of a leader in Egypt, second in command to Pharaoh.

How would Joseph wear his latest coat?

> **The Joseph Dream Vision.** *We climb up by the things beneath our feet. Take away life's challenges, and you take away its stepping stones. There is a connection between*

struggle and opportunity. Our refusal to give up keeps renewing aspirations and setting up new levels of potential for successful achievement.

When success comes, it carries new responsibility. Honor and integrity are as important when we arrive at new levels of success, as when we were struggling on small stages in early years. We may have increasing prestige and influence as we progress to larger responsibilities, but that only increases the need to be persons of integrity and honor.

Success carries responsibility. "Noblesse oblige." Nobility obligates.

Triumph had come at last for Joseph. End of struggle? No more hard places?

Joseph's agricultural policy worked well. Not only were Egyptians being supplied with grain from the reserve storage bins during years of drought, but people from nearby countries were coming to Egypt to buy grain.

One day when Joseph walked in to meet with a delegation of buyers from another country, he was surprised almost beyond belief. There were his ten older brothers! He recognized them, but because of the intervening years, his clean-shaven face, and coat of Egyptian authority, they did not recognize him. As soon as Joseph walked in, they all bowed to the floor, immediately. As his brothers were bowed, Joseph's boyhood dreams flashed in his mind. He could see the boyhood coat his father had given him which had set his mind with dreams and aspirations beyond those of his brothers. Then another scene rushed his mind. He could see his brother twisting his treasured coat in the dirt. He could see himself at the edge of the pit, pleading with his brothers, 'Please don't push me in there!' The acute memory of that experience was so vivid that, for an intense moment, he was back at the edge of the pit.

When that flashback ended, Joseph's brothers were still on their knees before him. It was his chance now to make them taste the pit. He could make them know humiliation, and regret the day they had sold him. He could make them go back home with no grain in their sacks. He had the power now.

But Joseph had an even greater opportunity. He could honor the trust his father had placed in him when he gave him that special coat with its distinctive identity, and when he had asked him to go find his brothers. He had an opportunity now to put the pit behind him forever and prove that he could truly close the door on the wrongs of the past, and open new doors to the future.

Instead of thinking of how he could avenge the wrongs of the pit, Joseph said quietly, 'Please rise.' Without revealing himself to his brothers, he drew up a sales agreement for grain, but also included a plan to get them to return for more grain, and to bring their youngest brother with them.

> **The Joseph Dream Vision.** *Joseph could never have been proud of himself if he had acted in revenge and sent his brothers back home with no grain. It would have crippled his self respect, diminished his honor, and belittled his success.*
>
> *When we get to that place in our journey story where we are a person of power and distinction, will we have truly earned it by our being big enough to be little and proud enough to be humble? Success endows us for new levels of responsibility and opportunity, in which many people will be depending on us to be big, and to address the future instead of being encumbered by the past. That's when we will win, not just respect from others, but self-respect. Whatever other title we might win in life, self-respect is the highest title we will ever earn and hold.*
>
> **We have a chance to live out a story we look back upon and be proud to claim as our own story.**

Shortages continued in their home land and soon the brothers returned to Egypt to buy more grain, As Joseph had required, their youngest brother, Benjamin, was with them. When they came in and bowed, and then stood before Joseph, there was his youngest brother, Benjamin. Joseph could keep his secret no longer. He asked all of the Egyptian assistants to leave the room, while his brothers waited in silence. Then Joseph went over and put his arms around Benjamin. His other brothers stood by, anxious and puzzled. With his arm still on Benjamin's shoulder, Joseph turned and said, 'I am your brother. I am Joseph.' Stunned silence followed.

Joseph went around and embraced each of his brothers, then came back and stood beside Benjamin. He said, 'My thoughts race back across the years and distance. I don't know what your thoughts are in this moment, but I can imagine. Perhaps it is hard for you to believe this is really happening.' Then Joseph explained how all the rejection, injustice, and adversity had been challenge opportunities in strange disguise to help bring about this unique moment. He said, "Don't be angry with yourselves that you did this to me, for God did it!" (Genesis 45:5) Later he repeated the reconciling words, "As for you, you meant evil against me, but God meant it for good." (Genesis 50:20 RSV) In those tough and tender moments, Joseph turned hurt and wrong into healing and promise.

> *The Joseph Dream Vision. When we keep on embracing the promise of the future instead of holding on to an unchangeable past, forgiveness is not all that hard. We may be amazed at how things which seemed to be only an end, can be turned into creative new beginnings. Positive expectancy creates a golden thread of purpose which gets woven into our story.*
>
> *When we stay positive, and when the journey is intense enough to turn into touchstone journey, we climb past invisible boundaries to higher levels of thinking, emotional strength, social grace, and achievement potential. Even*

though our struggles seem to contradict it, we can believe that some of life's most difficult journey can turn out to be for good.

Keep believing in possibilities.

It was an exciting moment when Joseph's brothers returned home from Egypt. As soon as they got within sight of the old olive trees surrounding the tents of home, and close enough that their father could hear, they began to shout, "Joseph is alive, and he is ruler over all the land of Egypt!" (Genesis 45:26) Jacob could hardly believe it, but after the brothers showed their father the lavish gifts Joseph had sent to him, he said, "It must be true! Joseph my son is alive! I will go and see him before I die." (Genesis 45:28)

Before Jacob began his trek to Egypt, he went to an old trunk where he had stored some treasured keepsakes. He raised the lid slowly. There was the coat of many colors he had given to Joseph many years earlier. He remembered the day Joseph's brothers had brought the torn, bloodstained coat to him, saying that they had found it in a field, and asked, "Is this Joseph's coat or not?"

"Yes," he sobbed, "It is my son's coat. A wild animal has eaten him. Joseph is without doubt torn into pieces." (Genesis 37:32,33)

Tears fell again on the coat as he held it in his arms in tender embrace. He knew what he would do with the coat now, he would take it to Egypt and present it to Joseph again.

Jacob carried that dual symbol of tragedy and blessing with him as he journeyed to Egypt. When Jacob approached his son, that coat was lying across his outstretched arm, and fell on Joseph's shoulder, as they embraced. Tears flowed down their faces. In a broken voice, Jacob said, 'Oh, my son, my son, I never thought I would ever see you again.' Then he turned his face toward heaven and prayed, 'O God of Abraham, God of Isaac, God of Pharaoh, and my God, thank you, oh thank you, for this very special day.'

Then Jacob turned to his son and said, 'Joseph, I saved your coat of many colors across the years as part of an unfulfilled dream.

Never did I realize the dream was still being fulfilled, and that I would have this opportunity to present the coat to you again. Truly, God has blessed you beyond anything you ever dreamed.'

Joseph reached out slowly and took the coat. He ran his fingers across the fabric and looked at his father and said, 'Thank you for saving my special coat all these years. I never knew what happened to it, but the memory of that coat has been a part of my life ever since. The confidence you showed in presenting it to me has helped me to believe in myself, and to feel there was a sense of purpose building in my dreams beyond anything I could see. In a sense, I have continued to wear that coat all across the years.'

> **The Joseph Dream Vision.** *As we walk on parallel journeys with Joseph, we can ask ourselves about the coats we wear.*
>
> *Is there a coat of hope and confidence which emerged in our dreams early in our youthful years, which never completely faded away, even in the pits? And what coat have we worn on some bitter and disappointing nights of our journey? Have we ever worn the coat of a new career, with exciting new energy, only to have it stripped away on life's auction blocks? When have we been expected to wear the coat of faithful duty? Have we ever worn a coat which seemed like a prison coat? What coat has helped us to interpret the strange experiences of life in honest and insightful ways? And have we ever been given a coat of importance and responsibility?*
>
> **We can wear all of life's coats with honor.**

When Jacob tenderly placed Joseph's coat of many colors in his hand that second time, now so many years later, the mystery of that moment must have been almost unbelievable. When we imagine Joseph standing there, looking down at that special coat, thinking back across the journey with thoughts that linked his touchstone journeys, we may finally know the answer to the question, "Should Joseph forget his dreams?"

Granddad waited for an extended moment, looking down at the glowing coals in the fire. When he lifted his head and looked at his special little audience, he said, "Stories have always played an important part in how we think. Joseph's story is one of the most important stories in sacred texts. It's a story about tough journeys and how to turn them into touchstone journeys. It's about turning problems into some kind of opportunity. It's about the future we ask for, not just once, or twice, but again and again until our unyielding dreams become our enduring request of life.

> **The Joseph Dream Vision.** *Should Joseph forget his dreams? There are always two factors, what life hands to us, and what we do with what life hands to us. It's true as the old saying goes, things turn out best for those who make the best of how things turn out. When we never stop giving our best to life, we never stop entering our best request of life. Not only should Joseph not have forgotten his dreams, neither should we.*
>
> ***It's always the right time to dream our best dream.***

CHAPTER FIVE

Back Up The Mountain

Were they to measure themselves by who they had been,
or by who they could become?

And when we fail, we know it's not time to quit trying,
but our time to go back up the mountain!

GRANDDAD WAS IN A PENSIVE MOOD AS HE BEGAN HIS AFTERNOON story. He said, "Sometimes stories get written by looking back on earlier days and seeing the significance of something back then which only fits into the puzzle after the broader framework and outline has come into place. It gets that way when I come back out here to the farm where I lived as a boy.

John Greenleaf Whittier did a reverse reflection on life like that and wrote a poem about it, entitled "The Barefoot Boy."

> Blessings on thee, little man,
> Barefoot boy, with cheek of tan,
> With thy turned-up pantaloons,
> And thy merry whistled tunes,
> With thy red-lip, redder still,

Kissed by strawberries on the hill,
With the sunshine on thy face,
Through thy torn brim's jaunty grace,
From my heart I give thee joy, –
I was once a barefoot boy. [1]

Reflectively, Granddad said, "I was once a barefoot boy, and in those days here on this farm, one of the hobbies we three brothers had was hunting Indian arrow points. Long before my ancestors farmed this land, American Indians were the ones who lived and hunted on this farm land. They had lived here long before a major migration from Europe to the new world began that changed where the Indians chose, or were forced, to live.

Again and again, migration has changed civilization's story. One such migration occurred many centuries ago when a surging flow of Hebrew immigrants left Egypt in search of a new homeland, led by a leader named, Moses.

When people wrote that story, they looked back on the life of Moses in terms of the progression of his story from when he was a baby, all the way up to the time when he brought the Ten Commandments down from Mount Sinai.

The story of Moses is one of the most dramatic stories of early human history. Like many stories about persons of notoriety, his story may contain as much legend as history. But who does not like to hear his story? It has become an epic dramatization of success beyond failure. It almost didn't happen. We would never have had his story, if it had not been for a great second effort in which Moses went, back up the mountain.

There are four major epochs in his story.

The first epoch tells how his life was dramatically spared when Pharaoh's daughter discovered a little basket floating in the river

---

[1]   John Greenleaf Whittier. "The Barefoot Boy"

with a little baby boy in it. It was Moses. It happened at a time when there was an edict that all Hebrew boy babies were to be killed because the Egyptians feared the Hebrew segment of the population was becoming too great. In order to save her little boy, Moses' mother devised a plan – float her little boy down the river in a little boat-basket to where the Egyptian princess would find and rescue him. Her plan worked. Moses was not only saved but cared for by his own ingenious mother and sister until he became old enough to go live at the palace of Pharaoh.

Moses was quite aware of his Hebrew roots and felt a special kinship with the Hebrew people, even though he was considered a son of the Egyptian princess. One day he saw an Egyptian overseer beating one of the Hebrew workers. Moses responded in an angry retaliation and killed the Egyptian who was mistreating his fellow Hebrew. But now, with his Hebrew loyalty revealed, his own life was in danger. For his own safety, Moses immediately fled from Egypt. He retreated to the desert country of Midian, where he found refuge with a priest named, Jethro, and became a shepherd. Jethro had seven daughters and Moses fell in love with one of them, Zipporah, who later became his wife.

Here is where the second great epoch began and stretched across many years. While Moses was following the life of a shepherd, he led his sheep to grazing ground on the slopes of Mount Sinai. One day, as he trekked the mountain terrain, he gazed in wonder at a strange kind of fire at a holy site. A bush was burning, but it did not burn up. He moved closer for observation. Then a voice came from the burning bush and said, "Moses, take off your shoes for you are standing on holy ground." He understood it to be the voice of God. Moses listened as the voice told him he must go to Egypt and free his people from oppression.

Moses put up strong resistance. Finally, however, he yielded to the call of the future and went back to Egypt to carry out his mission. It was a long and difficult task, but eventually the Hebrew people left Egypt, crossed the Red Sea, and escaped into freedom.

As they were escaping, it's easy to imagine that long procession of new immigrants, moving forward, leading sheep and cattle, pulling carts, and carrying basic possessions. They trekked for days before they stopped in the deserts of Midian where they could live in the foothills of Mount Sinai and gradually grow into a new nation.

The third epoch began when Moses heard God speaking again. There was no burning bush this time, but once again, as he stood under the shadow of the peaks of Mount Sinai, he heard the voice of God calling to him from those mountain summits of mystery, asking him to cut two stone tablets and bring them up to the peaks of Mount Sinai where he would write on them ten basic laws to guide his young nation.

You can say that the story about Moses going up a sacred mountain for God to write the Ten Commandments on tablets of stone was metaphorical. Even so, in your imagination, watch Moses as he goes to a young man named, Joshua, and urges him to go with him on his strange journey up the steep and rugged trails to the peaks of Mount Sinai.

You may, or may not, share Cecil B. De Mille's vivid dramatization of God writing on those stones with blazing lightning bolts, one after another, until the Ten Commandments were emblazoned on the two tablets of stone that Moses had brought with him up the mountain.

Even if that is beyond your imagination, you can easily imagine what was happening back at the wilderness camp where Moses had left his older brother, Aaron, in charge. After several days, the people who had made their dramatic exodus from Egypt, became restless in their identity. They went to Aaron and asked him to make them a God like the one they had known in Egypt. So Aaron called for a collection of gold items the people had brought with them when they left Egypt. Aaron made a form and poured the liquid gold into the form to make a golden bull – a 'god of Egypt.'

The next day when Aaron set the shinning golden bull up in the center of the camp, the people began to dance around it with great excitement. Then they put together a feast and celebrated. They felt like they were back in the familiar environment of their past.

Meanwhile, Moses was in the peaks of Mount Sinai, seeking insight into a new future for his people. In contrast to Cecil B. DeMille's, Ten Commandments movie version, in which God writes with lightning bolts, I like to think that, day by day, Moses carefully etched his insights and guiding rules on those two carefully selected slate stones he had laboriously carried up the mountain. When they were completed, Moses and Joshua began their descent back down from their mountain retreat, filled with hope for the future of the young nation. For so long, their full attention had been devoted to the exodus from Egypt. Now that they were free from a desperate past, they needed a template of ideals and standards to guide them to a promising new future. The journey back down the mountain proceeded with far more rapid steps than when they trudged up those steep inclines. In their arms they carried their two precious stones on which their future vision was carefully etched in Ten Commandments.

As Moses and Joshua neared the campsite, they heard sounds drifting up from the valley. Joshua stopped and said, "Listen. There is fighting in the camp."

Moses stopped. He listened carefully. "No," he said, 'it's not a cry of victory or defeat, but singing.'" (Exodus 32:18) They continued down the mountain, more rapidly now than before. When they got to the camp, Moses pushed through the crowd until he stood in the middle of the camp, right in front of the gold bull. Suddenly the music and dancing stopped, and the people stood motionless, staring at Moses.

'Where's Aaron?' Moses demanded.

Aaron moved forward slowly. Moses looked at him sternly and then pointed up at the bull. 'What's that?' he demanded in anger. 'I thought we had left Egypt!'

'But you were gone so long,' Aaron replied. 'The people didn't know what to do or think. They had to have something to believe in, so we collected gold and made this bull.'

Moses couldn't believe what he was seeing! An idol? In his camp? He glanced at the two tablets in his arms. One line on the stones said, "You shall not make yourself a graven image." (Exodus 20:4 RSV) Moses looked up at the gold bull. He glared angrily at Aaron. Then he turned to the people. He made no attempt to hide his disappointment, his hurt, his anger. Fury was in his eyes. The distance between the people's understanding of themselves and the ideals he had etched on the stones for them was so great that it seemed mockery even to read the commandments.

Why? Why was Moses so upset? A golden bull, a little dancing and music, a feast for the people – it all seemed such a little thing. But it wasn't little to Moses as he sought to shape the identity and future reference for his young nation. Who were they? What was their self-image? What was to be their reference? The past? Or the future? Were they to measure themselves by who they had been, or by who they could become? Were they simply to be relocated Hebrew-Egyptians? Were they going to achieve no more than transplant the religion and culture of Egypt into a new geography? Was that all they had struggled, dared, and risked their lives for? Or, were they to be a new people, with a reference to their own unique future as a nation of justice, ideals, cooperation, and a high respect for the sacred? Would they think most about the past they had escaped, or the vision of a new future that called to them?

It was a full identity crisis. Back in the days of planning for exodus the big words had been freedom, deliverance, emancipation. These concepts had motivated them to risk grave dangers and make personal sacrifices. But that phase was over. Now, the big words had to become justice, courage, faithfulness, cooperation, and community. Moses wanted a new tomorrow for his new nation in marked contrast to yesterday. And he wanted a new understanding of God – not something that could be represented by 'graven images' that people could make with their hands, but a new reverence for an unseen God.

Moses had etched a moral code for that vision on two tablets of stone, Ten Commandments, to guide them in living together as the beginning of a great new nation. All of these ideals seemed utterly betrayed by what Moses found when he returned to the camp and saw that gold bull. He was angry, humiliated, and discouraged. So, in his disappointment and anger, he threw the stones to the ground where, perhaps to his surprise, they shattered in pieces. It was an impulsive move, and he could hardly believe that they had broken into pieces, but it was done. Regret could never restore those stones or the precious words on them. In the stunned silence that followed, Moses stepped over the broken stones and walked away.

Can you imagine some of the advice Moses got that evening from the people who came to his tent to talk with him? 'Now, Moses, don't feel so badly. You were just upset. Everything will be all right. If you can't remember what was on the stones, we can just adapt some of the laws of Egypt and go right on. It's no big deal.'

But Moses knew differently. He knew they stood at an important identity crossroad. The diffusion of their identity and image would be disastrous to their courage, unity, and purpose-power. I can imagine Moses saying, in defiant and almost thunderous reply, 'It is a big deal! If that's all we are, if that's all we are dreaming for ourselves, we have canceled out the very purpose of leaving Egypt. We may as well have stayed. No! We must be different. We must define who we are by who we want to become, not by who we have been. We can't just be transplanted Egyptians. We, who would not be the slaves of Pharaoh, will we be the slaves of Pharaoh's gods? If we do not make a complete break with the past, we will have forfeited our future, for we will have lost our will, our vision, our reason for being. We must have an identity of purpose, sufficient to keep us pushing ahead in the face of even greater hardships and larger challenges than those we have known so far! Our freedom has just begun!'

The fourth major epoch was when Moses heard God calling one more time.

Changing the people seemed a bigger mountain than Mount Sinai. But it was out of his discouragements and identity struggle that Moses heard God speaking to him again, "Cut out two stone tablets like the first . . . Then in the morning go up Mount Sinai; stand and wait for me there at the top." (Exodus 34:1, 2 NEB)

Can you imagine hearing Moses saying, 'What? God, you have got to be kidding! After what happened, the contradictions, the humiliation, you expect me to try again?'

And God's answer was, 'Yeeesss.'

There was a chance the young nation might not listen to Moses when he came back down the mountain with a second set of commandments, but he knew he had to try. He had heard a call to go, back up the mountain.

So, Moses cut two tablets of stone like the first and set out on his journey, back up the mountain. There was no fanfare as he left the valley that day. Nobody was praising him as a dreamer or hero now. Some, instead, may have said, 'Crazy fool! Who does he think he is? Doesn't he know when he's finished?'

But Moses was no idle dreamer, as he trudged up those hills again. He was simply a man who believed in his goals beyond failure – a man who dared to take big risks again. It was a second chance at failure, but it was also a second chance at success!

Moses was representative of those who conquer fear of ridicule. Yes, it was a dumb thing to do – throw those stones down. Moses may have regretted his actions deeply. But instead of being demoralized by such an embarrassment and letting the past define the future, he was motivated by the opportunity to prove what can be done on the other side of failure.

Moses was representative of those who get angry, but who turn their anger into extra drive for success. Such persons can be counted on to make an even greater contribution in the long run because they care enough to be that upset.

So do not ask only, 'Did Moses get angry and throw the stones down?' Ask instead, 'Why did Moses get so angry that he threw his precious stones down?' And the answer is not that it was an act of resignation because he didn't care. On the contrary, it was an act of defiance because he cared so very much! Those broken stones, then, did not lie at the feet of a defeated, crippled, despondent, complaining, has-been leader. They lay at the feet of a winner, a true leader, who would never accept defeat without giving his best effort another chance to win. He had to go, back up the mountain.

The figure you see disappearing again into the distance was not just the same man returning again – he was a greater man! His new resolve had been refined by the fires of disappointment and signaled by renewed dreams.

The commandments Moses brought down the mountain the second time may have been the same as those he brought down first, but the man carrying them was not the same! He was a man who lived with an un-relinquished dream for his young nation. He was a man who believed in himself beyond failure, beyond rebuff, beyond embarrassment, beyond anger, and beyond trying only that which is easy.

What would Moses have been able to do with the first set of commandments if he hadn't broken them? Would he have had the personal and defining power to make them instruments of great leadership and unyielding vision? We cannot know. What we do know is that the second set of stones, even if they were the same as the first, were more powerful instruments because they were carried in the hands of an intense man of extra resolve and inner strength, who dared to go, back up the mountain.

The Exodus and the Ten Commandments are defining meta-phors of Israel's identity. They have remained powerful signals by which those who stand in the legacy of Moses define and measure themselves for great second effort.

Is it possible that Moses was more legend than history? Even if his story was created by later storytellers, what a story! And what a great representative for all of us whose success must be on the other side of failure, where success is achieved by extra resolve and persistent second effort, in which we dare to go, back up the mountain.

When Moses made that great second effort, it was not for his own personal recognition. He went to his people the next day and said, "You have sinned a great sin, but I will return to the Lord on the mountain – perhaps I will be able to obtain his forgiveness for you." So, Moses returned to the Lord and said, "Oh, these people have sinned a great sin, and have made themselves gods of gold. Yet now if you will only forgive their sin – and if not, then blot me out of the book you have written." (Exodus 32:30 – 32)

It was a plea for the future of his people, over and above his own legacy. Moses did not live to see his nation cross over into their future land. There is no gravesite for Moses, no historical monument, and little historical evidence that he was the leader of the Exodus, but there is his story! And we have it because Moses dared to go, back up the mountain.

It is those stories any of us write, on the other side of our failures, which show who we really are. Whatever represents broken commandments at our feet, we dare not give up before we make a great second effort and go back up the mountain.

When Moses descended from the mountain peaks of Mount Sinai, he brought down Ten Commandments, as a revelation from God, to guide the future of his young nation. A metaphorical new "Moses" has come down from the mountain peaks of civilization's lengthening story of tragedies and triumph with a new Big Ten. Out of the long progression of human knowledge, a new guiding template has been distilled into ten words to define the way forward as a new sacred. These words call upon us to define our future by the qualities that lead to a new promised land of wholesome living. The new Big Ten qualities guide the ways we relate to one another by being kind and caring, honest and respectful. They help us to cooperate together by collaboration and tolerance, by fairness and integrity. They define our summit of qualities as people of diplomacy and nobility. Borrowing from the giant step forward as provided by the Ten Commandments of Moses, as we advance forward in the progression of civilization's collective identity, the Big Ten Universal Qualities form a framework for identity that can lead us into a new promised land.

We honor both the tradition of Moses and the teachings of Jesus when we bring the Big Ten Universal Qualities down the mountain into our everyday story. And when we fail, we know it's not time to quit trying, but our time to go back up the mountain!"

Granddad looked from side to side at his treasured porch audience as he said, "When I think about our need to go back up the mountain, I think of a poem by the poet, Frank L Stanton, and his unique way of meeting challenge – Keep a-Goin. Listen in.

> If you strike a thorn or rose,
>   Keep a-goin'!
> If it hails or if it snows,
>   Keep a-goin'!
> 'Taint no use to sit an' whine
> When the fish ain't on your line;
> Bait your hook an' keep a-tryin' -
>   Keep a-goin'!
>
> When the weather kills your crop,
>   Keep a-goin'!
> Though 'tis work to reach the top,
>   Keep a-goin'!
> S'pose you're out o' ev'ry dime,
> Gittin' broke ain't any crime;
> Tell the world you're feelin' *prime* -
>   Keep a-goin'!

When it looks like all is up,
    Keep a-goin'!
Drain the sweetness from the cup,
    Keep a-goin'!
See the wild birds on the wing,
Hear the bells that sweetly, ring,
When feel like sighin', sing –
    Keep a-goin'! [2]

---

[2] Frank L Stanton. "Keep a-Goin'"

CHAPTER SIX

Beyond Cover-Ups

His finest hour was when he dared to tell a story.

GRANDDAD LOOKED UP FROM THE MANUSCRIPT LYING ON HIS LAP and launched into his next story.

"Names and stories sometimes become metaphors. Among them are metaphorical names like David, often referred to as Israel's greatest king, and Bathsheba, the beautiful woman who lured David into his foulest sin, and Nathan, the court prophet who dared to challenge David's wrong. Filmmakers have presented David and Bathsheba's story in dramatic movie roles. But, it's Nathan's story that needs to be told anew in our time, not on the big screen, so much as in the quiet penetrating power of metaphor. It's a story about a risk-taking hero who represents the courage to put integrity above personal advantage. It's a story about account-ability – about a future, beyond cover-ups.

It has been said that when you are writing about a hero and you have both the facts and the legend, write the legend. In David's case, legend and sketchy facts blend together to begin the dramatic story of a red-haired shepherd boy who was discovered by the prophet, Samuel, and anointed to be king while he was still only a boy. But another story tells of David's encounter with the giant, Goliath, and how he won against impossible odds, which resulted in his being chosen to be king. Yet another story tells how David was a court musician and played for the depressed and unpredictable, King Saul, until jealousy enraged the king and David had to flee for his life. Later the fugitive returned and became King of Israel and led the army into so many invasions, conquests, and plunders that, as a result, Israel became a powerful and wealthy nation.

So, King David became a celebrated leader. He had many wives, and beautiful women as his concubines. It's not that he lived with all of them as wives, some were political alliances, but they were his personal harem. He was wealthy. His people worked hard to build a fabulous cedar palace for him in Jerusalem. He continued to build up the military and launch oppressive conquests. After the battles, he brought back gold and bronze, young slaves, and levied taxes on the conquered nations, which they dared not refuse to pay.

One Spring, David sent Joab, the general of the army, out to fight the Ammonites. But David stayed behind in Jerusalem.

The storyteller of long ago said, "One night he couldn't get to sleep and went for a stroll on the roof of the palace. As he looked out over the city, he noticed a woman of unusual beauty taking her evening bath." (II Samuel 11:2)

Was there no private place to take a bath? Or was the display of her physical beauty intentional? We don't know for sure, but what we do know is that David watched and then sent someone to find out who she was and discovered that she was Bathsheba, a soldier's wife. The soldier was Uriah and he was away with the army. How convenient. So David sent for her and she came and spent the night with him. Then she returned home.

The next thing that happened was, David got a note from Bathsheba – she was pregnant. Now what? David knew his affair with a soldier's wife wouldn't make good public relations. But he could fix that. It would be an easy cover-up – just get Bathsheba's husband to come home from the battlefield and sleep with his wife for a few nights and then everyone would assume that he was the father of the baby.

So, memo number one to Joab, general of the army, "Send me Uriah the Hittite." (II Samuel 11:6)

'You sent for me? I am at your command, sir!' Uriah said, when he was presented to the king. 'How may I be of service to my king?'

David said, 'I wanted to know firsthand from one of the soldiers just how the battle is going. I'd like to hear your report.' David listened as Uriah talked about the troops and battle plans. 'That's great, and I know all of you soldiers are doing your very best for your country. While you are here, I want you to take a few days leave – go home to your beautiful wife and relax for a while. You've earned it.'

'Oh, thank you, sir. That's great,' Uriah responded. He bowed to the king and departed.

It wasn't long before David called in a servant and said, 'I want you take this bottle of wine down to Uriah's house. Good soldier. Deserves the best. Tell him it's with my compliments for the fine job he is doing.'

But soon the servant returned with the wine and said, 'Uriah is not at home.'

Listen to the original storyteller describe what happened.

"But Uriah didn't go there. He stayed that night at the gateway of the palace with the other servants of the king.

When David heard what Uriah had done, he summoned him and asked him, "What's the matter with you? Why didn't you go home to your wife last night after being away for so long?"

Uriah replied, "The Ark and the armies of the general and his officers are camping out in open fields, and should I go home to wine and dine and sleep with my wife? I swear that I will never be guilty of acting like that."

"Well, stay here tonight," David told him, "and tomorrow you may return to the army."

So Uriah stayed around the palace. David invited him to dinner and got him drunk; but even so he didn't go home that night, but again he slept at the entry to the palace.

Finally the next morning David wrote a letter to Joab and gave it to Uriah to deliver. The letter instructed Joab to put Uriah at the front of the hottest part of the battle – and then pull back and leave him there to die! So Joab assigned Uriah to a spot close to the besieged city where he knew that the enemies' best men were fighting; and Uriah was killed along with several other Israeli soldiers.

When Joab sent a report to David of how the battle was going, he told his messenger, "If the king is angry and asks, 'Why did the troops go so close to the city? Didn't he know there would be shooting from the walls?' . . . then tell him, 'Uriah was killed, too.'"

So the messenger arrived at Jerusalem, and gave the report to David. "The enemy came out against us," he said, "and as we chased them back to the city gates, the men on the walls attacked us; and some of our men were killed, and Uriah the Hittite is dead too."

"Well, tell Joab not to be discouraged," David said, "The sword kills one as well as another! Fight harder the next time, and conquer the city; tell him he is doing well."

When Bathsheba heard that her husband was dead, she mourned for him; then when the period of mourning was over, David sent for her and brought her to the palace and she became one of his wives; and she gave birth to his son. But the Lord was very displeased with what David had done." (II Samuel 11:9 – 27)

Case closed? Well, not quite. In fact, not at all. There was Nathan, one of the court prophets. David and Bathsheba's story may have been a secret to other people, but not to Nathan. He knew the whole despicable episode. Joab, the general of the army may have known what was going on, too, but he would never tell. His whole battle plan had been woven into the intricate plot and many were killed just to get one soldier killed.

You can see Nathan in your imagination now, pacing the floor, back and forth, or walking along secluded paths, or sitting down on a big rock, getting up and shuffling around a few steps and then sitting down again, praying, thinking, processing one scenario after another.

In his mind he was debating – *who is a king? And who am I? Dare I challenge the king on what he has done? Is a king above the law? Or is he accountable to a higher law – a law so high that nobody is exempt from its standards? Can a king do anything he pleases? Are soldiers dispensable merely to satisfy his way of life – just to cover up his affair? When is a king out of order? And when is it more than a matter of just being out of order – when is it a matter of being such a serious flaw in character that it undercuts his leadership role and personal respect – a matter that destroys his integrity and authenticity? When does a king cease to be a steward of entrusted power and become a user of power to his own ends?*

On another day, you can see Nathan meeting David in the corridors of the palace, and David being cordial to the court prophet, just as though nothing were wrong and nothing had happened. Nathan responds with equal cordiality, but the next moment he is back in his thoughts and saying to himself – *what a hypocrite I am. I have to confront him. He is as accountable to God as I. And, I am accountable to God to remind him of his accountability.*

Then you can almost hear Nathan arguing with himself – *but I like being a court prophet. What other prophet in Israel isn't envious of my position and opportunity? It means I have arrived. I have status in my moment in history. But if I am where I am and have no integrity, if I am not willing to take risks to carry out the role of a true court prophet, then I don't deserve to be here. I don't even deserve the title of prophet, for the very essence of my role as a prophet is that I am willing to do what is right even if it is to my disadvantage or personal loss. I am supposed to confront wrong wherever I see it. So I am no more exempt from fulfilling my role than David is from his. Both of us must give full accountability. Both of us are rubbing up against a touchstone which will tell whether we are real, or phony. If I don't confront him with his wrong, I am bowing to convenience and to my own weakness just as much as he has bowed to his. And, yes, I am scared, but this is a test. If I don't prove myself worthy in this moment, I will have rubbed up against the touchstone and found to be only fool's gold. And if I don't demonstrate character in my high-profile moment of important decision, how can I expect other prophets, in their respective roles, to be persons of honor and integrity? I have to tell him. I just have to!*

But then again, Nathan felt a bit of honor just to keep quiet and protect the king against scandal. He reasoned — *I could even be helping the king and nation in that way. Maybe that is the honorable thing to do — spare David's reputation and spare the nation of turmoil. I can just close my eyes and keep quiet. I can show how loyal I am. I could do more harm than good to disclose the truth.* It felt good — thinking how noble it would be to sacrifice his own feelings for the good of his nation. Nobody would ever know. *Shouldn't I make that sacrifice? Is that too much to ask?*

On the other hand, he knew that by hiding the truth to protect David's honor, he would have to sacrifice his own honor. He wasn't just up against David — he was up against himself — against his integrity. Sparing David was an option, but not if he wanted to be true to himself as court prophet. There simply was no easy choice.

He knew what he had to do. *But how? How can I get past David's defenses and possible anger? How can I get past the blindness that protective self-interest creates? How can I keep from being thrown out as court prophet, maybe even murdered, like Uriah, a second cover-up?* Finally a burst of insight comes. *I know — I'll use a metaphorical story. Stories have been the vehicle for truth for hundreds of years. A story will penetrate or bypass his safety-zone defenses.* Immediately, Nathan felt the exciting energy of hope and relief from fear and the depression it causes.

Nathan got an appointment with the king. On the way to meet the king, you can hear Nathan rehearsing what he is going to say, and reinforcing his decision. *'I have to do it. I don't know if others know David's secret, but I know. It is so unworthy of a king — so despicable — so devious and atrocious that nobody should be allowed to cover up so foul a set of deeds. I have to follow through and tell him.'*

The ancient story says,

"So the LORD sent the prophet Nathan to tell David this story.

'There were two men in a certain city, one very rich, owning many flocks of sheep and herds of goats; and the other very poor, owning nothing but a little lamb he had managed to buy. It was his children's pet and he fed it from his own plate and let it drink from his own cup; he cuddled it in his arms like a baby daughter. Recently a guest arrived at the home of the rich man. But instead of killing a lamb from his own flocks for food for the traveler, he took the poor man's lamb and roasted it and served it.'

David was furious. 'I swear by the living God,' he vowed, 'any man who would do a thing like that should be put to death; he shall repay four lambs to the poor man for the one he stole, and for having no pity.'

Then Nathan said to David, 'You are that rich man!' . . . For you have murdered Uriah and stolen his wife.' (II Samuel 12:1-7, 9)

David dropped his head and waited in a stunned silence. His secret was not a secret. The baby was his. He had ordered that Uriah be killed. There was no one else to blame. Then he confessed to Nathan, "'I have sinned against the Lord.'" (II Samuel 12:13)

Nathan assured David that God had forgiven him. He said, "The Lord has forgiven you, and you won't die for this sin. But you have given great opportunity to the enemies of the Lord to despise and blaspheme him, so your child shall die." (II Samuel 12:13, 14)

The baby became very sick and David fasted, and prayed that the baby would live. But, seven days after the baby was born, it died. David went to the Tabernacle to pray. Then he turned his attention to Bathsheba again. Later Solomon was born to David and Bathsheba.

In that quiet confrontation, Nathan not only demonstrated the power of metaphor as a valuable vehicle of insight, but he had also elevated the role of prophet, including all spiritual leaders, as one of the important touchstone roles of all time. It was a choice – to be in the hall of fame, or in the hall of honor.

It is the role of prophets to live in creative tension with their age. And it is the role of religion to nurture prophets. Prophets are the debaters of their age. And though the spirit of the times may lend itself to an easy compliance with low standards, betrayals, and cover-ups, no prophet is exempt from taking Nathan's kind of risks if he or she is to have integrity. And none of us is exempt, either.

All of us – scientist, politician, business person, minister, journalist, writer, peace corps worker, educator – all the priests of learning and leadership, all of us are accountable for what we do with our knowledge and insights. We are accountable to challenge the ways of life which lead to wrong and injustice, to dishonesty and deceit. We are accountable to challenge whatever turns back the clock of true human progress. It will require not just thinkers, but re-thinkers. It will require disassembling some traditional paradigms so new ones can emerge. At times that may require courage, risks, struggle, even personal sacrifice. It will always require a commitment to excellence and integrity. And it will require a willingness to be accountable for the opportunities given into our hands in this new age of enlightenment.

To be true to the prophetic tradition that Nathan modeled, today's prophets must measure up to being honest about the progressive nature of knowledge, especially science and technology and the new powers its tools have put in our hands. Unfortunately, religion has not had a good record in its regard for science and new knowledge, thereby seriously compromising its leadership. We are accountable for what we learn in the laboratories of knowledge, and for making those changes which show we have a higher respect for true knowledge than for our own self interest.

We cannot point a finger at others, and at history, without personally admitting that it is so easy for us to hide behind words, craftily created to disguise our true self, so that we look better than we really are. It's so easy to tell only half of the story and leave off the straightforward answers which would reveal who we really are. It's easy to blame leaders who twist information to serve some personal and political agenda, and not face up to just how easy it is for any of us to be a 'yes' person, to the boss at work, or to friends in order to keep up our image and friendships, or to keep our jobs.

All of us stand before the bar of human community and are accountable for the story we write in our time in history. Data collection and massive digital information are no hiding places. Our responsibility to the human family only increases in our new digital-information age. This is true for all priests of learning, and especially for writers, whose influence may extend a thousand years into the future. It is the writer's responsibility to be a carrier of a noble vision of our humanity as we redefine who we are, can be, and should be, in desirable alternatives. All of us should be trying to find answers to the big questions about our humanity and our future, where our accountability is expanding because of the new power our tools have put into our hands which expand our potential.

So, I am a teller of stories. I am not a theologian or historian. I am a teller of stories which are important carriers of insight and vision. Although the stories I tell come from yesterday, I tell them in terms of our accountability today, and as a call from tomorrow. They help us define ourselves in terms of an overarching vision that goes beyond the traditional views of these stories, beyond mythology, beyond rigid adherence to sacred texts, To have integrity with my place in the story, they must be a part of an open-ended, knowledge-based vision for the human family.

If you read more of David's story, you will discover that David was no saint. Far from it! His invasions of other nations were violent. Heartbreak followed. His armies killed without mercy. They plundered and carried valuables back to Jerusalem. Subject nations had to pay heavy taxes. Again and again, David led his armies out to take over territories and bring back gold, silver, and slaves. And sometimes he stayed at home – you know that story.

While it may be extraneous to the story I am telling, it is not extraneous to those of you who have studied Shakespeare in college, you know that all Shakespeare needed to do to have more material for his tragedies, beside that of his own times, he could have just gone to the Bible. The stories surrounding David's invasion atrocities and personal evasions and cover-up are despicable. The graphic details are all there – deceptions, revenge, rape, murder, and brutality to subject people. Read some of the stories in II Samuel, chapters eleven through nineteen, if you dare. They are not pretty. But this open reference to David's larger story, keeps me from telling a whitewashed story. And where could anyone have gotten the idea of the divine right of kings? Just figure it back.

So, have we made progress in civilization? It's easy to say, no, and cite stories from our own time that parallel the subversive activities of David's time to illustrate that conclusion of, No. While we learn from the past, we must be even more focused on learning from the future! We must try new ventures and learn in process as we give our best dreams their best chance to happen.

It is a time of great opportunity for us to learn from the past, adjust to new factors in our progressive knowledge up to now, and then dream a more honorable dream for the future."

In an obvious reflection upon the prolonged monologue he had just given, Granddad lifted both hands in a kind of, 'perhaps' gesture and said, "Wow! I may be laying it on too strong. Tell me that I have stopped telling a story and have begun philosophizing, and I will admit it. But, it's when stories turn into new insight that they become crossover scenarios for our learn forward moments. And those kinds of stories are important, especially in our time in history. Maybe it's too much like one of my class lectures. But unless we learn from the worst pages in our story so far, we will not take maximum advantage of their lessons for our time in history, when we need so much to find new vision for a better future which can make this the greatest age of promise the world has ever known. My hope is that each of us can write a story in which we a learn forward as our response to a call from the future.

Our ethics is progressive. Our stories have a bigger base and carry a larger responsibility now. The arena is no longer one nation, but a family of nations – one earth family. Our indebtedness to make tomorrow better than yesterday is a stewardship responsibility for every person on earth. And how we treat each other now, extends to a declaration of human rights for all people. Each of us gets to have a place in the story and to take our dream-vision to a whole new level, where we measure by the gold standard set forth in the story of Nathan, the prophet who dared to tell a story.

Nathan lived a long time ago, but he helped established the role of a true prophet for all time. It is not just the role of the prophet to challenge wrong – the true prophet champions the right. True prophets help salvage the good out of the brokenness of the ages and then reinvest the accumulated and tested wisdom of painful passage into a wiser and better future.

Prophets – priests of learning and leadership, all of us, are stewards of insight from a vision of the future. We must see things, not just as they have been, or as they are, but as they ought to be, and go to work to maximize our growing network of resources and abilities that give better ways, a chance to work in our world.

But back to the story. In the old story, Nathan was not ousted from his position as court prophet. Perhaps he had gained the respect of David as never before. Years later, he was able to show his loyalty to David and help him keep a commitment he had made to Bathsheba. He had promised Bathsheba that her son would succeed to the throne. Nathan helped avert an insurrection that made it possible for Solomon, Bathsheba and David's son, to succeed to the throne.

But that was not Nathan greatest legacy. His finest hour was when he dared to tell a story."

CHAPTER SEVEN

Unfinished Dream

He dreamed of a kingdom of faith and brotherhood
that cut across all lines and boundaries.
"The man who uses well what he is given shall be given more,
and he shall have abundance."

GRANDDAD LEANED BACK, PUT HIS HANDS ON THE ARMS OF THE chair and smiled, as he looked around the semi-circle of his grandchildren, now waiting for him to tell them another story here at the farmhouse where his own stories and dreams began. He said, "When you were children you used to say, 'Granddad, tell us a story.' I loved it then, and I love it now when I get to tell stories to you. This old porch is becoming more and more special to me every time I have the privilege of meeting here with all of you and telling stories from yesterday that help us define our best tomorrow.

Today, I want to let our imagination help us connect some dots in the story of one person who helped the human family take a giant step forward in an unfinished dream! You have heard about this philosopher-teacher. His name is Jesus. They often just called him Teacher. He was from Nazareth.

It was early morning, and still dark, in their little house in Nazareth, when Jesus got up and lit a candle. By the time he got together some travel clothes and supplies, and ate some food, daylight was beginning to break across the distant mountains, northeast of the Sea of Galilee. He had told everybody good bye the night before, so they were still asleep. After extinguishing the candle, he slipped out the door and closed it quietly behind him. With steady footsteps, he made his way down the street and then onto the road leading south. It was the beginning of a two-day trek of twenty-five miles each day, to visit with his cousin, John. He had heard stories that John was drawing unusual crowds as he talked to people down near the edge of the Jordan River. It was time to find out for himself what was drawing so many people to listen. If he pushed right on all day long he could be there before nightfall on the second day.

It was the surprise of the day when John saw his cousin walk up. They embraced each other in glad reunion. "You're looking great," John said to Jesus. In turn Jesus said, "And so are you. This desert life must be good for you." John began immediately to take Jesus around and introduce him to his disciples and friends.

There was considerable contrast between the two cousins. John was rustically clad in leather and fur, suitable for desert camping. His attire was not at all like the elaborate robes he would have been wearing if he had become what his father had expected him to be, a priest, like himself. But John had chosen a desert way of life and very simple clothes.

Jesus was dressed in a deep burgundy robe. A golden yellow silk cord made the robe fit closely around his waist. But their difference in dress did not keep them from sitting by the campfire long into the evening and talking. They had so much in common. Each of them was entranced with the idea about leading people into a new age – a kingdom of a different kind, where the social order would be inverted. Common people, rather than the rich and powerful, would be the leaders of a new a kingdom without borders. Humility and kindness would rank above tradition, religious authority, money, and position.

John had seen how religious leaders of his time were so tied to the past they couldn't take hold of the future. He had been in line for the priesthood because his father was a priest, but he just couldn't see himself doing that. He had to break free. So he made a complete break and came out into the wilderness, chose some disciples, and began preaching on the banks of the Jordan River. His message was simple and direct – a kingdom of heaven is coming soon. People were so eager for a new day that they came out in throngs to hear him, and listened with excitement and hope.

Like John, Jesus was thinking about making a big turning point in his life. Day after day he worked as a carpenter, sawing, smoothing boards, making furnishings, driving pegs, laying stones, and building houses. All the while, ideas were surging in his mind about being a leader of a new approach – living a simple life as a kingdom, not in a distant heaven, but here on earth. He kept thinking about a faith-oriented kingdom in which people would commit themselves to a life of kindness and love – not some set of religious rules set by the quasi-political system of the Temple. He dreamed of a kingdom of faith and brotherhood that cut across all lines and boundaries – a self-chosen kingdom. Anyone could belong to it and develop the better side of humanity.

What an exciting idea! What a challenge! But would he dare to lead it? Would he dare to launch out like John? Maybe he could join with John in some way – be one of his disciples. He knew he had to find an answer.

Each day as he listened to John's sermons, new ideas energized his mind. At the end of one of John's sermons, people were coming down to the river to be baptized as a witness to their acceptance of the new kingdom of heaven vision. Jesus was among those who came down to the river and waded out in the water until he stood in front of John, ready to be baptized. John hesitated. He hadn't expected that. He knew the quality of Jesus' thoughts and ideals.

John felt that if either of them should baptize the other, it should be Jesus baptizing him. But Jesus insisted that he wanted to receive John's baptism. So John baptized his cousin in the Jordan River.

It took only a moment, but it was a defining moment. Jesus had announced himself to a new way of life – to a new mission. But what would he do, and how would he go about it? He had to think about it, alone. So he told John he would be away for a few days.

It was beside a smaller stream, far from the Jordan River, that Jesus set up camp, out in the wilderness, all by himself. He may have camped under a rock cliff or built a small shelter from branches of trees. He may have sat at the edge of the stream, listening to the ripple of the water as it tumbled over the rocks, while big dreams tumbled in his mind. What mattered most was that he could be alone to think and plan. Mostly, he didn't sleep or eat – just walked among the trees along the stream. At night he may have gazed up at the stars, praying and thinking, laying out first one scenario and then another as a way to go about his plan for a kingdom of heaven on earth.

Could he go back and join with his cousin? Would he launch out on his own as a teacher, and, like John, have his own disciples? How many would he need, and how would he select them? Would he take his message to the cities and villages? Would he go to the synagogue and preach there? Would he seek high visibility?

Jesus' biographers told about the temptations he faced and how he rejected them – do dramatic things, like turn stones into bread, glide down from the pinnacle of the temple in front of people, become a political figure. In the end he rejected those and decided he would never play to the grandstands and become just a crowd-pleasing sensationalist. Instead he would be a teacher with a few disciples of his own and go about telling people to accept and love everybody no matter who they were or what they had done.

After many days in the wilderness, Jesus was ready to go back to see John. When he got back to the camp-site by the river, no one was there. The blackened coals in the campfire were cold. When he went to a nearby village to inquire, he learned the distressing news. John had been arrested.

Jesus set out for Nazareth, immediately. Perhaps he could find two of John's disciples, Andrew and Peter. At the edge of the Sea of Galilee he found them. He was glad to see them. Jesus walked down to the pier and asked immediately about John.

"He has been arrested," they said.

"I have heard. But, why?" was Jesus' quick question.

They told about John's preaching and how he had said it was not right for Herod to marry his brother's wife. Herod was so upset by that charge that he had John arrested and put in prison. "What can we do?" was Peter's question.

"I know what we can do," Jesus said, "We can join together and make sure John's message doesn't stop."

Mark tells the story. "Jesus and his companions now arrived at the town of Capernaum and on Saturday morning went into the Jewish place of worship, the synagogue, where he preached. The congregation was surprised at his sermon because he spoke as an authority, and didn't try to prove his points by quoting others – quite unlike what they were used to hearing!" (Luke 1:22)

After that, Jesus went back to Nazareth and preached in the synagogue there. Then he returned to Capernaum and preached in the synagogue regularly.

But he did not limit his preaching to the synagogue – more and more he began to preach from the fishing pier, or even from a boat, because such great crowds began to gather to hear his message. At other times he would preach from a mountain side.

Matthew, one of his disciples, gave a composite of his mountainside sermons, and we can read that synthesis now in Matthew's book as, The Sermon on the Mount. In great respect for his teachings, people began to call Jesus, Master.

As his popularity grew, people began to look back on his life and tell stories about his boyhood, even about his birth, and how unusual he was from the beginning. Yes, the stories blended in with the mythology of those times, just as mythological stories of all time have been told about great leaders. Stories were circulated as anecdotes in an attempt to understand his popularity and success.

We have not been left to our imagination about that unfolding story. Four different writers have told these stories of Jesus. Each of them incorporated metaphor as they looked back years later, and told the story from different viewpoints.

One story of the early life of Jesus was about a strange visit of three wise men who came to see Jesus when he was just a little boy and left him gifts of gold, frankincense and myrrh. Well, what do you think Joseph and Mary may have done with those gifts – used them for themselves, or thrown them away? Probably not.

So it's okay to imagine that one day, a few years later, when Jesus was a young boy, his mother sat down beside him, put her arms around his shoulders and drew him close. A tear trickled down her face as she said, 'Your father is sick, very sick, and these could be among his last days. He wants to talk to you. Could we go in to see him now?'

'Come in, son,' Joseph said to Jesus. 'Sit beside me. And, Mary, would you now bring that special basket, please.' Mary walked over to a tall cabinet that Joseph had built for her. She opened the top door of the dark stained cabinet which sat in the corner of the room. Carefully she lifted down a basket from the top shelf and brought it to the bedside. Joseph said, 'Now, Jesus, would you please unfold the cloth in the basket.' Carefully Jesus pulled back the cloth. Joseph said, 'There, Jesus, is something you have seen before, but, of course, you do not remember, because you were just a little boy when you saw it. But, now take a look at what is in the basket.'

Jesus reached in and picked up a small box. He opened the lid of the box carefully. 'It's Myrrh,' Jesus said, as the spicy aroma filled the air.

'Yes,' Joseph said, 'And what else is there?'

Jesus reached into the basket and drew out a beautiful small vase. He opened the top. 'And this is frankincense, to be sure,' he said. 'What's it for? Where did you get these?'

Without answering the question, Joseph said, 'Pull back the layer of cloth in the bottom of the basket.'

Jesus pulled back the layer of the cloth and exclaimed, 'It's gold. Lots of it! Where did you get it? Whose is it?' Jesus asked. He looked into the fixed gaze of his father, and then his mother, waiting for an answer.

Slowly Joseph answered. 'I will tell you. But you must remember this before I tell you. There is great mystery in the story that goes with what you have just seen. I don't understand it all. It is possible the story is only in its beginning, and could be worth more than the gold, frankincense, and myrrh. I hope you will remember that, son.'

'How can I forget?' Jesus said. 'You have aroused my deep interest.'

'It's all yours,' Joseph said. 'Your mother and I have saved it for you ever since that mysterious day when three strange men appeared at our door. They said they had followed a star which led them to our house. They asked if a baby had been born. When they were told you had recently been born, they wanted to see you. They said their God had led them and that you were to be somebody special. Before they left, they presented some gifts – the gifts you have just now seen. They said they were astrologers from another country. We have never seen them again, but we have never forgotten those brief and mysterious moments. We kept the gifts for you. So now, we think it is time for these gifts to be presented to you on their behalf. You will discover how to use them.'

'I am grateful to you for saving them for me,' Jesus said. 'And I will keep the gifts and treasure them.'

'No. No,' Joseph said quickly. 'That is the one thing you must not do. We have kept them for you, but you must not keep them. That would make them almost worthless, especially the gold. You must find some way to use them to help you become that special person they talked about. You see,' Joseph said haltingly, 'There are other stories which make Mary and me respect the mystery of the appearance of the strangers and their gifts. Perhaps Mary will tell you those stories later. But for now, you must begin to look for ways to use the gifts so their real worth will come forth.'

'Can you tell me some of the other stories?' Jesus asked.

Joseph looked at Mary, then turned back to Jesus. 'I'll tell you one more, and then Mary may tell you others, later. When you were eight days old, we carried you to the Temple for a service of dedication. We were so young and happy and felt so blessed as we carried our baby boy to the Temple. As we were walking so proudly across the courtyard of the Temple, we noticed an old man watching us very intently. Soon he called to us and we stopped. He came nearer. It was the old prophet, Judah. Everybody knew about Judah, and knew he had said, again and again, that he would not die until he had seen God's special person. Judah looked at you with such admiration. Then he said, 'May I hold him a moment?' When he held you in his arms, he looked up and began to speak reverently, '"Lord,' he said, 'now I can die content! For I have seen him as you promised me I would. I have seen the savior you have given to the world. He is the Light that will shine upon the nations, and he will be the glory of your people Israel!'" (Luke 2:29-32) My son, I cannot tell you more now. Nor do I know the meaning of what I have told you. I trust that in time you will discover what it all means.'

People liked to tell another story about Jesus in his early years, about the time he got lost from his family on a visit to Jerusalem. He was twelve years old when the family decided to go on a pilgrimage to Jerusalem and to visit the Temple. They toured the city and Temple for two days. At the end of the second day, they went out to the edge of the city and put up camp for the night, before beginning the walk back home the next day. It was a larger family event, so the children tended to stay together in their own groups for fun and play. But when dinner-time came, and Joseph and Mary gathered all their children around, Jesus was not among them. 'Where's Jesus?' his mother wanted to know. The answer from each of them was, 'I don't know. He hasn't been with us.' The immediate conclusion was that he had gotten lost in the city. There was nothing to do but set out immediately to retrace their steps to find him. All night long they searched. When morning came they went to the Temple to ask if anyone there had seen him. Then they saw him, talking to some of the teachers. They rushed up to Jesus and, after giving him a big hug, chided him for not keeping up with them. 'We've looked all over the city for you,' his parents complained.

Jesus wondered why they would have searched anywhere else but here at the temple. "Didn't you know I would be here at the Temple, in my Father's house?" (Luke 2:49)

Beyond the stories people were telling about Jesus, they treasured the stories he was always telling in his talks, often as parables and metaphors.

As big crowds came to listen to Jesus, a lot of people were trying to figure why he was such a special teacher. That's when they remembered and told those early stories, especially the one about his being found at the Temple talking to the scholars of Jewish law. When they told that story, they wanted to show how he had been smarter than the average person, even in his early years.

Some people were saying that Jesus stood in the shoes of prophets, like Isaiah. Others thought maybe he was the long awaited Messiah. Some thought he represented a new Moses, because he not only redefined Moses, but defined his own message in terms of leading guidelines for new times.

When Jesus was baptized by John the Baptist, it showed that, like John, he was ready to define himself, not by the past, but by a new future. He called upon people to dream of a new beginning – a kingdom of heaven on earth. The old guidelines of, eye for an eye, could never create a new tomorrow. Revenge only created resentment, anger, and more revenge. It needed to be replaced with new measures. Be fair. Respect others. "Do unto others as you would have them do unto you." It was his new vision. John the Baptist had been killed for his views, and although Jesus knew how risky it was for him to be as bold as John, he continued to proclaim the new sacred. People flocked to hear his message. They had been ready to listen to a man living in the wilderness, wearing leather clothes and living off the land. Now, they were ready to listen to a man who dressed in a nice robe, but got sand in his sandals and was down to earth enough to wash his disciples feet. So many people flocked to hear him that, at times, he had to climb up on a mountainside, or speak from a boat, to keep from being to crowded by his admirers.

Jesus had many admirers, but he also had jealous enemies. Some accused him of being against Moses and the law. That was like burning the flag. Temple authorities and Pharisees felt threatened by him. They said he was a traitor to the true faith. They were ready to get rid of him, to kill him, if they must. He knew it. His disciples knew it. Time was running out. His enemies were closing in on him.

Jesus wanted to have one final dinner with his disciples before it happened. Some of them thought no one could ever kill him — that he would perform some miracle. Some wanted him to escape to another country. But, no, he would not run. His own courage and integrity were at stake. At the dinner table, he passed around a cup of wine and made it into a metaphor of the suffering he was about to face. He wanted to know if they could drink from that cup, too? There was no easy choice for any of them. After dinner Jesus went out among the olive trees to spend the night. That's when soldiers came out to arrest him, betrayed by one of his own disciples who knew where he would be that night.

The next day, Jesus was subjected to a trial, after which they took him out to the edge of the city and hanged him on a cross.

They left him there to die. A friend came, and took him down from the cross, and buried him in a tomb.

Now his disciples faced new questions. Not, just, *"Who was Jesus?"*, but, *"Who are we?" Should we just forget about Jesus and go back to our old ways?* The influence of this magnanimous person was still with them after the death of their Master Teacher. They got together in Jerusalem and tried to figure out if they had a future. That's when their courage was expressed in the symbolism of the Feast of Pentecost and they pulled together and said, 'Let's keep his vision going.'

And the story goes on.

When Fulton Oursler wrote the story of Jesus in a book that has sold millions of copies, he called it, *The Greatest Story Ever Told.*

In my own way, across many years, I have been trying to tell that story of the manhood of the Master. And to update the progression of that story to, and for, the cell phone, digital, information, molecular age, I have gleaned insight from many books, ranging from history to science fiction, from theology to self-development books that define a bold vision of the future. Out of that search to advance the noble qualities Jesus lived out in his lifetime to our time, I now believe those ideals and the kingdom of heaven vision of Jesus for the promise of the future can be focused into ten very important guiding words, the Big Ten Universal Qualities. I believe these ten words refocus the dreams Jesus called, a "the kingdom of heaven on earth," into a framework of identity that can guide the human family to new tomorrows. We are the beneficiaries of the progression of knowledge and its tools up to our time when that endowment of the ages, so nobly advanced by Jesus, opens a new doorway to the greatest age of potential the world has ever known.

When Jesus put that framework of identity into a story, he told about three persons who were entrusted with money to invest by their master, while he was away in another country. The man who was given the largest amount to invest, soon doubled it. And so did the man who had been given less than half that much. But the man who was given the least, discounted the opportunity he had been given. He buried it to keep from losing it.

When the investor returned, the man who had been given the most to invest, reported on the investment. It had doubled. Likewise for the person with less than half that much to invest, it had doubled. But the man with the smallest amount, brought back only what he started with. That's when the master took his money back and gave it to the man who had been most successful in using his resources. Jesus summarized that story as a principle of life, saying, "the man who uses well what he is given shall be given more, and he shall have abundance. But from the man who is unfaithful, even what little responsibility he has shall be taken from him." (Matthew 25:29 TLB)

It was a parable story in which Jesus talked, as he did in many stories, about being a winner at life by giving your best to life as your request of life. His own story led the way. He dared to give his best to life, especially when he faced many challenges to his idealism, and finally the life and death challenge. That approach to life was at the heart of the teachings Jesus taught by the sea, and backed up in his own story of courage and honor!

When we extend this approach to our own place in the story, the challenge to is to make sure we choose, and dare, to live at the leading edge of the progression of humanity's greatest qualities, and give our best dreams their best chance to happen!

Albert Schweitzer did that in his own choice to give his life as a medical missionary in Africa. It was while he living out that courageous story that he made his own discovery about who Jesus was, and, in turn, who the person was that he wanted to be for his place in the story.

> As one unknown and nameless He comes to us,
> just as on the shore of the lake, He approached
> those men who knew not who He was. His words

are the same: 'Follow thou me!' and He puts us to the tasks which He has to carry out in our age. He commands. And to those who obey, be they wise or simple, He will reveal Himself through all they are privileged to experience in His fellowship of peace and activity, of struggle, and suffering till they come to know, as an inexpressible secret, "Who He is. [3]

In his biography of Jesus, when Matthew introduced the stories Jesus told about successful living, he said, "Jesus left the house and went down to the shore, where an immense crowd soon gathered. He got into a boat and taught from it while the people listened on the beach," Matthew 13:1-3 TLB

Little wonder that people crowded in at the edge of the sea to hear him, they came to hear the teacher whose own story has now become, the greatest story ever told.

So the question is not just, 'Who was Jesus?' but who do we choose to be in the progression of the human story? Dare we have the courage to envision and announce a new tomorrow, the way Jesus did? Dare we continue to dream of a kingdom of heaven on earth? And, dare we to be one of today's disciples of Jesus, who say, 'Let's keep his vision going.' What if we choose to live by the Big Ten Universal Qualities, as our place in the story of an unfinished dream?"

Granddad's voice changed as he said, "And now it's lunch time All of you are to be guests of your grandmother and me at our local restaurant. There you are likely to have questions and comments about this morning's story, and I will welcome them, along with your own insights from your journey stories.

When we return after lunch I want to tell you about a banquet where Matthew told his own story about the influence of the Master Teacher on his own story.

---

[3]   Albert Schweitzer. *Out of My Life And Thought.*

CHAPTER EIGHT

The Banquet

What I know is that he saw possibilities beyond limitations.

WHEN THEY HAD ALL GATHERED ON THE PORCH FOR AN AFTERNOON story session, Granddad began by saying, "The story I am going to tell now lets you attend a special banquet. It's a story that highlights the humanity of Jesus. You can see a side of Jesus that is hidden behind all the theology which has kidnapped his story. By adding enough imagination to the vignettes the original biographers told, you get to be there and see the real human Jesus as others saw him in their time.

The banquet was at Simon's house. It was an elaborate stone house up on a hillside with a large patio on the eastern side, over-looking the Sea of Galilee. Inside, there was a long atrium with six tall columns, three on each side. Large palms accented the grandeur of the atrium which had now been made into a banquet hall, with a long table down the center. Many people had been invited to come to a special banquet in honor of a person who had made a tremendous difference for good in their lives. They had been invited to honor Jesus of Nazareth, teacher, healer, and special friend of so many!

Jesus felt the warm congeniality of the occasion as soon as he arrived and was greeted by Simon, and by friends, as they gathered in. Some of his disciples had come, and like Jesus, mixed among the guests as they arrived.

The atrium was a blur of conversation when Simon tapped on a small clay bell to get the attention of all the guests. He invited them to gather around the long table in the atrium, with Jesus being invited to come to the head of the table to take the place of honor. Jesus moved slowly to his place and, in turn, others began to take their places around the large table. It was Simon who remained standing when others took their places at the table.

Simon's opening words of welcome were given in a cordial, welcoming manner. 'I am so very pleased that all of you have come to be guests in my house. When I invited you I told you why I wanted to have this celebration. But I want to say again that this occasion is to be a testimonial dinner in honor of a special person who has made such a difference for good in the lives of all of us here. I speak of Jesus of Nazareth, our very honored guest. And, not only am I so pleased that you have come, I am also pleased that some of you accepted my invitation to speak and tell something about Jesus, and why he is such a special person to you.

When the time comes for this, I want to begin by telling about my own experience. Then I have invited my good friend, Zachaeus, to say a word. After that, Bartimaeus will speak. Peter wanted to say something, but I told him I knew how shy he is, and how hard it would be for him to get his words together.' Spontaneous laughter erupted. Then Andrew followed the irony by saying, 'Nobody knows better than I how shy my brother is, so if you still want somebody to speak, I will speak on his behalf. After all, I am the one who introduced him to Jesus. Since then – well, you know how timid Peter is.'

'Yes, we know,' someone shouted, and everyone laughed again, all of them knowing full well Peter never needed anyone to speak for him. "Mary Magdalene is here and will make a special tribute to Jesus. Then I've invited Matthew to close out the tribute.

And, 'Jesus, I know you are always ready to say something, but this evening we will just let you listen. I know that won't be much easier for you, than for Peter to keep quiet. But even in your silence, you will still be speaking, for your presence here speaks to all of us. Kind Sir, we are honored to have you here among us. And we thank you for letting us speak out of our respect and gratitude.'

But of course, all of this is to follow our dinner together, for which all of us are so deeply indebted to my dear wife, Hannah, to Lazarus, and especially to his sister, Martha. 'So, Hannah and Martha, with our very special thanks for your gracious help, you and your helpers may begin serving.'"

Across the years, all of us have had the privilege of imagining this occasion because early writers told us many things about Jesus and how he enjoyed the company of people and having dinner in their homes. So, as one of today's writers about Jesus, I have taken the liberty of pulling back the curtain a little more, through imagination, so we can be there at the banquet in Simon's house, in honor of Jesus, and listen in.[4]

So, now that they have all finished their dinner, let's just stand over to one side and listen. Simon is about to tell of his special indebtedness to Jesus. He looked around to see where his wife was. She had been serving the dinner, but now was standing over by one of the columns. In a very tender and almost tearful voice, he said, 'Hannah, would you come over here and stand with me a moment?' Simon reached out and took her hand and then put his arm around her waist. He said, 'There was a day when I thought I would never be able to do this again. I remember the day I left my home and family – stricken with leprosy – couldn't even hug and

---

[4]   Story – Matthew 26:6-13. Mark 14:3-9

kiss her goodbye – couldn't even touch her because of the terrible disease I had. It was the toughest day of my life as I just turned and walked away to go out and live in isolation. My world closed behind me that day. You can imagine my amazement the day Jesus came out to the cave where I was living with other lepers, and reached out to take my hand. When I respectfully declined, he told me I was cleansed of my terrible disease. I could hardly believe he would even dare to come out to see me, much less offer to touch me. But when he said I no longer had the terrible disease, it was almost beyond belief. But, I looked down at my hands. I looked at my arms. The sores were gone! He was right. I was well! I reached out to take his hand, saying, 'Thank you! Thank you so very, very much!'

I don't know how it happened. He hasn't told me yet. What I know is that he saw possibilities beyond limitations. Even if there had been other healing forces involved over time, he was the one who came out to tell me I was healed. So, however it happened, it's enough to know that it was true. So, here I am! Look at me. Good as new. I have my business back. I have my health back. And I have my family back! I don't need to say any more for you to know, why I wanted so much to have this banquet in honor of Jesus and to have it here in my home, where he made it possible for me to return.' Simon reached over and took his wine glass and raised it for a toast. 'To Jesus! Friend! More than a Friend!' His voice broke at the end of his words. He looked down a moment to get his composure back. He lifted his wine glass higher, then took a sip of the wine and sat down.

A moment of respectful silence followed as Hannah walked away. Zachaeus stood up, but looked down for a moment and then said, 'I'm afraid to look at Jesus right now, afraid he might say, Zachaeus, come down.' Everyone laughed and then began to applaud his clever reference to that day he had climbed up a tree to see Jesus, then came down and was surprised when Jesus suggested that he would like to be his guest for dinner. 'You remember, don't you, Jesus?' Zachaeus said, as he now finally looked over at him. 'Those were the first words you ever spoke to me. Please don't say them now, because this time I might not respond as quickly as I did that day I came sliding down the tree. People say I came down so fast that it pealed the bark off the tree, never has grown the same since. However that might have been, I do know I responded immediately for I was really pleased. You not only said for me to come down, but that you would like to go home with me for dinner. I don't know how you knew my wife was such a great cook. She is just that, as you could tell when you ate at her table.

That day, after we finished eating, we sat at the table and talked. Matthew and I had been good friends, fellow tax collectors for Rome, and I had heard him talk about you. So, I already knew how understanding you were about those who worked for Rome. I also knew how you thought it was a matter of personal choice each of us had to make about right and wrong, not just what the letter of the law says, but what is right. I remember telling you that if I had made any unfair tax assessments, I was ready to correct them fourfold and that I was ready to start helping the poor with up to half of my possessions. Do you remember what you said, Jesus? I do. You said, "Today salvation has come to this house." (Luke 19:9 RSV) And then you gave me a very high compliment. You said that I was a son of Abraham. It was such a gracious title and I really didn't deserve it. But I certainly didn't forget it. Those were healing words. It was a moment of restoration of my faith. Now, I really had something to live up to!

So, my friends, let me give you a word of caution. Don't let this man invite himself to dinner at your house, unless of course, you want to change your life. Somehow he does that for you, makes you want to rise to your best and to be compassionate toward others.

I thank my good friend, Matthew, for his kindness and friendship to me. I thank you, Simon, for inviting all of us to come so we can say a special thanks to Jesus. So to you, Jesus, thanks. Thanks so much! And now, Jesus, if you want to, sir, you can say,

Zachaeus, come down, and I will obey once again.' Everyone burst
into laughter and applause as Zachaeus bowed toward Jesus, raised
his glass in a toast, and then took his seat.

It was time for Bartimaeus to speak. He stood up and reached
out his hand in a searching manner and said, 'John, would you
please lead me to the place where I am to speak.' John hesitated.
Bartimaeus said, 'Come on, John. Where are you?' Bartimaeus was
still blindly reaching out his searching hand. John picked up on the
little drama and came over and took Bartimaeus by the hand and
led him over to the speaker's place.

'Thank you, John. And now, don't go far away, for I will need
you to help me back to my place again. No, no. Of course, I won't
need you to help me back.' And all of you know I didn't need
John to help me find my way here. I just wanted all of you, myself
included, to remember how it used to be before Jesus made such
a tremendous difference in my life by restoring my sight. And,
Simon, I'm with you; he didn't tell me how. I remember Jesus telling one lady, after her health was restored, that it was her faith that
made her well, that by seeing herself as healthy again, helped her
to become healthy. So, how it happened, I don't know, but that it
happened, I do know. I can see!

I had been sitting by the side of the road that day as Jesus was
leaving Jericho with his disciples and a large following of people.
When I heard it was Jesus, I began to call out to him. People tried
to keep me quiet, but I just kept on calling until he heard me. He
asked that the man who kept calling, come to him. So I began to
find my way. People stepped aside as I made my way. He could see
that I was blind, by how haltingly I made my way to him. Even
so, he asked me what I wanted. I said, "Master, let me receive
my sight." (Mark 10:51 RSV) Then, ever so confidently, he said,
"Go your way; your faith has made you well." (Mark 10:52 RSV)
Immediately I could see! I could see! I was so excited that I guess
I didn't listen too well. He said, 'Go your way,' but I went his way.
I joined the crowd and followed him, and have been one of his

followers ever since. I am glad that I got the chance to speak on this occasion as one of the persons who has the opportunity to express my public gratitude to him. And now, I had better go my way.' He lifted the glass and waited for others to lift theirs. 'To you, Jesus, sir, my highest esteem, my deepest gratitude, and my visible respect!'

After the applause diminished, there was a long pause. People began to look around. Mary was to be next. Where was she? Simon stood and looked around, but he didn't seem concerned. He looked beyond the columns and said, 'Mary, it's your time now.' Simon turned to the people at the table and said, "Mary didn't want to say anything; she just wanted to do something. I don't know what it is, she didn't tell me, but we can be sure if Mary does it, it will be special and unique. That's Mary's way – said she wanted to do something to honor the person who never sought honor for himself. "Come on in, Mary."

Mary came in from the side and down by the columns. She was so beautiful as she came walking across the atrium, her flowing blue dress accenting her black hair and dark complexion, carrying something in her hands. She made her way to the front and stood behind Jesus. Then she took the top off a beautiful bottle of perfume, got down on her knees, and began to dash the perfume on Jesus' feet. Immediately the fragrance filled the whole atrium.

Just then, one of the disciples rushed over and took her by the arm and said, 'Mary, don't you realize what you are doing? Don't you realize how much that perfume cost and you're just pouring it on his feet?'

Mary stopped and looked at him for one disgusting moment, then began pouring it again, even more lavishly than before. 'Does it matter that I choose to pour it on his feet? And, I don't care how much it cost,' she said. 'The more it costs, the more it helps me to say a special thanks to the person who gave me back my confidence and pride – just accepted me for who I was. I owe so much to him.' She looked up at Jesus and smiled. Then she stood up, leaned over and gave him a kiss on the cheek and turned and left. As she departed there was a burst of applause that just kept going, on and on. Jesus was among those who kept the applause going, standing and turning toward her, so that, as she left, he turned her tribute to him into a tribute to her, and her beautiful spirit.

Matthew's time was next. He waited a moment and then rose slowly and walked over to the place designated for the speakers. He looked at Jesus and said, 'I know, sir, that you had assumed that if one of your disciples spoke, it would be Peter. Right? But, I talked him into letting me be the spokesperson this time. Well, that's almost right. I told him that if he didn't let me speak, I was going to double the taxes on his fish. That's when he said, you go ahead and speak.' Laughter followed the well-taken jest.

'Jesus, kind sir,' Matthew began, 'I am not at a loss for words – just at a loss for where to begin. I have listened to you speak many times and often you began with a story as a parable. I'm not sure I can do that. So I will just begin with a simple story, my story.

To begin, I will say that you walked into my life through the door of friendship. That is to say, when I first heard about you, I was needing a friend, really needing one. I didn't need someone who could tell me about all the religious laws, what to do, what not to do, I knew that.

From the time I became a member of the synagogue as a boy, I learned the law. Then, when I began to work for Rome, the synagogue threw me out of its membership because of their rules. I was considered an outcast by the most religious people in the community. I was no longer welcome at banquets like this, weddings, and other social occasions. People were bitter toward me, as though I were a traitor. The bitterness became reciprocal. All I had done was take a job working with Rome. I was the same person who previously had been accepted. But I was out.

Needless to say, I felt only disgust and disdain for such narrowness and conceit, such arrogant spiritual superiority. I now know they were religious, but not brotherly. They knew how to keep their religion pure, but not how to make it inclusive and redemptive. So I was glad, very glad, I was no longer a part of their religious snobbery, with their street corner judges, handing out sentences of exclusion.

So, yes, I was needing a friend. Jesus, you became that special new friend. I needed someone to show me how to get beyond being bitter about being ejected from the synagogue because I didn't fit all their little rules. I needed someone to help me get on with life, to know how to trust again, how to forgive those who hated me, how to give love away. You did that for me because you didn't reject me first. You knew I worked for Rome. And while that made it hard for many people to accept me, it was not that way for you. Many feel so oppressed by Rome, that they are filled with resentment and hate every time they see a Roman soldier walking through our streets as part of the occupation army. And they resent anyone who collects taxes for Rome.

I can't forget one of your teachings about how to treat soldiers from Rome. Be kind and considerate. And believe me, Jesus, it was your teachings which have meant so much to me. Anyway, you talked about the soldier, how he had the right to demand that a person carry his pack for him a mile, and had better do it. But what you said was that, if a soldier asks you to carry his pack a mile, instead of resenting that demand, you should make it into an opportunity to be kind, and carry his pack, not just one mile, but carry it a second mile, just to show that you care about him, far from home, and want to be kind and helpful. As a result, what you get from carrying that pack is an inner gratification from rendering a service. I had never heard anyone talk with any kind feelings for the soldier just as a fellow human being. And I also heard you say, just turn the other cheek when someone slaps you. I don't think you meant that so much literally as you meant for us to return kindness for insult and hate – like being kind to the soldier, or anyone else who might not be all that nice to us. Instead of retaliating and making enemies, make friends. And, I've seen you do that, sir. And I'm trying to learn to do it, to be kind to all those who find it so

easy to be unkind to me, now that I work for Rome. You helped
some of those here to find healing for the body. You helped me
find healing for the mind.

It may be that I respect your teachings more than most people.
They seem to apply to my own experience so much. I've heard you
advise us to pray for our enemies, try to make them into friends.
That's not easy, but it helps. I've heard you say that we are to treat
others like we want to be treated. And I've heard you talk about
forgiveness, about how there is to be no limit to forgiveness, that
we are to reach out to all persons and care about them, not give
up on them; they could become best friends. You not only talked
about that, you did it, and I happened to be one of the lucky ones
to whom you did that!

It's so easy to be hot and angry inside, and to vent it on others
at the least provocation. I remember that day we were on our way
to Jerusalem. I was a junior disciple, but Jesus, you sent me and
another disciple ahead to make reservations in a Samaritan village.
But when they learned we were headed for Jerusalem, they refused
to let us stay there. I couldn't believe it. It made me angry. When
we came back and told you what the innkeeper said, we asked if
you wanted us to call fire down from heaven to consume him.
But, very calmly you said, "Ye know not what manner of spirit
ye are of." (Luke 9:55 KJV) What I will admit now is that I was
angry and defensive. But that is out of character for you, Jesus. It
is such a betrayal of the qualities you want us to keep reaching
for – compassion, tolerance, kindness, forgiveness, patience, gen-
tleness, consideration, loving, understanding, fair, just, thoughtful,
humble, unselfish – not religious words, just words which define
us as bigger than other people's littleness. I've never forgotten that
incident. It helps me define myself anew by the qualities you have
modeled before us.

I especially remember that earlier day at the fish market. I was
helping the fishermen weigh in the fish they had caught on the
Sea of Galilee, and then collecting the tax on that day's catch. You

came walking up with Zebedee and his sons, James and John. Peter and Andrew were with you. When I kidded and said something about your being a fisherman too, Peter spoke up and said, 'He's a fisherman, all right. Only difference is, he catches people.'

That's when you said, 'That's right and I'm trying to catch one today.' You looked at me and said, 'Matthew, I want you to be one of my disciples.' And I said, 'Jesus, you got to be kidding. You don't want me. I'd be your biggest liability. You know how unpopular I am around here. And you know how angry I can get so easily.'

But you said, 'I'm not kidding and I'm asking you now to join us.'

And I said, 'Well, I won't kid either. If you want me to be one of your disciples, I will be glad to be caught in your net. And I would like to begin by having all of you come to my house for dinner.'

So, I invited some not-so-religious people who still dared to be my friends. In fact, the occasion wasn't too different from this one, except it was much earlier. You were just beginning then. But what I am leading up to is this. Some of the Pharisees heard about it and criticized you for going to my house as a guest for dinner, said you had gone to eat with tax collectors and sinners, put us both together, as though one equaled the other. I can laugh about that now, but it bothered me then, made me disgustingly angry. But that didn't bother you. When you heard what they said, you used a metaphor and said, "Those who are well have no need of a physician, but those who are sick." (Matthew 9:12 RSV)

Matthew continued. 'If I ever write a book, and I am thinking about it, it will be about you. I sat here thinking how all these testimonials ought to be put together some day. The things you said as we sat on my veranda talking, and as all of us traveled together – I would like to gather them all together. There ought to be a book about you with all your teachings in it. You keep challenging us to reach up for our highest level of excellence, no matter what has happened along the way – to turn each experience of life into a positive quest, as the way to win, even when we lose, to be bigger than other people's littleness. So often your teachings are about just that. I remember your talking about that old saying, "love your neighbor and hate your enemy". But you turned it around and said, "Love your enemies and pray for your persecutors; only so can you be children of your heavenly Father, who makes his sun shine on good and bad alike, and sends the rain on the honest and the dishonest. If you love only those who love you, what reward can you expect . . . what is there extraordinary about that?" (Matthew 5:43-47 NEB) Extraordinary – that's what you made us feel like we wanted to be. Genuine. Trustworthy. Honorable. You made life seem like a zestful quest for excellence! To me, and I am sure to all others here, you are the Prince of Excellence!

So, yes, I want to write a book which lets others know about this leader of vision, who helps us find a new tomorrow beyond yesterday's hurt and disillusionment, who restores hope and confidence.

Now, my friends, I have followed Jesus around to many places and listened to his teachings many times. And I have seen his great love and compassion as he has healed the sick, and always it was done ever so humbly and without fanfare or showmanship. And even now, as we honor Jesus at this banquet, he is probably ready to tell us to stop, and say no more. It's so unlike him to seek any praise or honor. On the contrary, he has advised, "When you do some act of charity, do not let your left hand know what your right hand is doing; your good deed must be secret, and your Father who sees what is done in secret will reward you." (Matthew 6:34 NEB)

Jesus has a different way of looking at things. For instance, he thinks caring about other people comes before keeping the law, that if you get that right, then you will already be fulfilling the best of laws. When the elders of the temple came up to him and asked to know about his authority, he talked about being flexible and open to new ways of seeing things; that those who are tax collectors and street girls may know more about caring, than those who are authorities on keeping the laws of Moses. This is how he responded to the chief priests and elders at the temple. He said, "Truly I say to you, tax collectors and harlots go into the kingdom of God before you." (Matthew 21:31 RSV)

It's possible to be so caught up in keeping the laws of Moses that we leave out tolerance and caring about others. Even if you have your religion just right, but don't have tenderness, warmth, and flexibility right, you betray what the law is about in the first place. What's important is helping others to be their best selves, not just getting them to comply with all the religious rules. Being caring is harder to live up to than keeping the law. Caring adds warmth and tenderness, strength and consideration into the way you relate to others, and if you have that, you have already fulfilled the law of Moses. You see, those of us here, who may not fit all the criteria of religion, can be as genuine, or even more genuine and caring, than those who keep every little detail of the law of Moses. And that's what Jesus expects. That's a big, tough challenge to live up to for any of us. Still, I keep trying.

I have just one more of his teachings I want to lift up. You see, all of us here have been changed by Jesus, but it hasn't always been sudden. For some of us, the change has been a process over time in which the energy of healing ideas have begun to work in our minds. I've felt that kind of energy, not in some sudden event, but while I have been following him and learning from him. And so I remember one of his important teachings in which he talks about wonderful things happening as an ongoing, dynamic process. He said, "While you are asking you will receive; while you are seeking, you will find, and while you are knocking, the door will be opened to you." [5] It's a process over time. I certainly was seeking. And while I was seeking, I found a new beginning.'

Lifting his wine glass he said, 'So, Jesus, here's to you and your special friendship to me, and to all of us!' Mathew held the wine glass up and continued. 'We salute you with our words, with

---

[5]   Matthew 7:7 Translated from original language.

highest respect, and much appreciation. We salute you with this, our privileged occasion. You are indeed our honored and esteemed guest! We do not know what the future will be, but we know it will be different, better, richer, more fully what it should be because we have been privileged to be with you on the journey.' Everyone followed Matthew's example as he sipped the wine. They set their glasses down and began an affirming applause. Matthew gladly waited.

'Simon, all of us are grateful to you for making it possible for us to have this time together. You gave me the privilege of bringing this very special banquet to a close. So I want to close now by asking that all of us say a prayer together that Jesus has taught us. We've remembered it, so let's all join in together. And, Jesus, may we have the privilege of having you lead this prayer?'

They stood quietly and joined in when Jesus began to say, "Our Father which art in heaven, Hallowed be thy name. Thy kingdom come. Thy will be done on earth, as it is in heaven. Give us this day our daily bread. And forgive us our debts, as we forgive our debtors. And lead us not into temptation, but deliver us from evil: For thine is the kingdom, and the power, and the glory, for ever. Amen." (Matthew 6:9-13 KJV)

Matthew did write that book. Oh, I know, it may have been written later in his name, and as though one is looking back on the story and can see it in a larger context, but to me it's Matthew's book. There's no bitterness in it – only respect and admiration for the Master Teacher he was privileged to know as a special friend and to honor at a banquet at Simon's house. As a disciple, he was there when Mary came in and poured perfume on Jesus' feet. He remembered what Jesus said, "The story of what she has done will be told throughout the whole world." (Matthew 26:13)

CHAPTER NINE

Damascus Road

What was troubling his mind
had to do with his being a part of a religion
which had no room for tolerance, reason, and change.

AFTER A BREAK, GRANDDAD BEGAN THE NEXT STORY SAYING, "I want to tell you about Paul, the world citizen who put the story of Jesus on the map of the Mediterranean world.

When you tell a story in terms of history, it's different from when you tell it in terms of metaphor. While the data base must be the same, the freedom is greater when you can draw metaphors from the story. That's how I tell stories, and how I want to tell a story about Paul — as both history and metaphor, but more as metaphor. It's about a boy who boarded a ship in Tarsus to go off to college, and then, on to a strange journey, and out of that, to become a world citizen.

The city of Tarsus is one of the oldest cities in the world. It has a continuous history for thousands of years. Tarsus is a river city in a fertile plain where their industries reach far back into yester-years. They were known for their fine linen, made from flax, and

for their tents, made from goat hair. The people who lived there
when Paul was young were from a mix of Jewish, Roman, and
Greek backgrounds. Paul's parents were Jewish. Their religion
was a strong expression of Jewish culture, steeped in authority and
tradition which exacted strict rules and codes on its devotees. It
carried a strong reference to the rules from the past, which were to
be obeyed, lest one betray God and sacred traditions.

Beyond the influence of his Jewish home, the culture in which
Paul grew up was largely Roman and Greek. It was a culture which
valued learning and the arts. It bore the influence of a shipping
culture. Business and commerce were important parts of life. Ships
regularly left the harbor for Egypt, Greece, and Rome. It was a
culture where far away places could be reached by going down to
the dock and boarding a ship.

It was the port at Tarsus where Paul boarded a ship, bound for
the port nearest to Jerusalem. Paul's Jewish parents went down to
the dock with their son, watched him go on board, then waved
goodbye, with sadness and pride – pride that their son was going
off to college to study Jewish religion, under the tutelage of the
celebrated rabbi, Gamaliel, in Jerusalem. As the ship slowly moved
down the river, Paul waved goodbye from the deck until it entered
the waters of the Mediterranean Sea, headed for the nearest port
to Jerusalem.

Jerusalem was restless in those days. The very popular Jesus of
Nazareth had been killed, but his disciples were carrying on his
work with growing influence. Many influential leaders felt the
followers of this new Way were disloyal to the Jewish faith. So the
established religious leaders began persecuting those who were
following the disciples of Jesus. As a young student, with Jewish
loyalty, Paul was soon caught up in the movement. The protests
turned violent. When an angry crowd began to stone one of the
most devoted young followers of the Way, named, Stephen, Paul
was there and watched the horrible death.

Not long after that, Paul joined in and became one of the

leading protesters. The hostile protests had the support of the religious hierarchy and Jewish law. Soon followers of the Way were being arrested and put in prison. It became so dangerous for members of the new movement, that many of them had to flee from Jerusalem and go to Damascus. Paul had now become so deeply involved, that he secured papers which authorized him to travel to Damascus and arrest these refugees from the law and bring them back to Jerusalem to stand trial. It was an unfortunate mix of religion and law into a violent concept of what constituted right.

But on his way to Damascus, something unusual happened. Judging from Paul's account of that later, we can see how the violence in his religion was in acute contrast to the goodness of the followers of Jesus. In vivid metaphors, Paul described a dramatic moment on his journey. He said, "As I was on the road, nearing Damascus, suddenly about noon a very bright light from heaven shone around me. And I fell to the ground and heard a voice saying to me, 'Saul, Saul, why are you persecuting me?'

'Who is speaking to me, sir?' I asked. And he replied, 'I am Jesus of Nazareth, the one you are persecuting.'" (Acts 22:6-8)

When we follow the story as extended metaphor, we know the Damascus Road was more than just a road from one city to another, and the light that Paul saw was more than sunlight – it represented new pathways of insight. The road was in his mind. What was troubling his mind had to do with his being a part of a religion which had no room for tolerance, reason, and change. The papers Paul carried, on his way down the Damascus Road, represented religious authority in concert with political power. Paul, and his entourage were given authority to arrest key leaders of the Way and bring them back to Jerusalem in chains, where they would be tried under the tyranny of their religion and its laws, and without mercy to those who betrayed those beliefs.

But another part of the Damascus Road was about openness to new ways of thinking. In this motif, hope, love, caring, and understanding were represented in real time by the followers of Jesus.

They dared to live by an overarching faith, instead of rigid adher-ence to a religion of authority, steeped in tradition. Paul had heard people talking about this new faith, perhaps even by his teacher, Gamaliel, who often spoke in sympathy with the new Way. The road was in his mind and emotions that day as the noonday sun was shining down on him. He stopped abruptly. He heard a voice, as though Jesus himself were speaking to him and asking him, 'why are you persecuting me?' Paul went blind and stumbled to the ground. He lay there with no answer, except to get up and find his way to Damascus and try to make sense of what was happening.

In Paul's time, writers had their own dramatic way of telling stories. They used dreams and visions as a way to define how people got their best insight. In our time we tend to say, 'I've been think-ing a lot about ...' But in Luke's dramatic style of writing, dreams and visions were mediums of insight. He said, "Now there was in Damascus a believer named Ananias. The Lord spoke to him in a vision, calling, "Ananias!"

"Yes, Lord!" he replied. And the Lord said, "Go over to Straight Street and find the house of a man named Judas and ask there for Paul of Tarsus." (Acts 9:10, 11)

When Ananias first entertained the idea of meeting with Paul in an overture of open diplomacy, it didn't take him long to reject that idea. *'You mean, go talk to the enemy — that terrorist of believers, who even now, I hear, has papers to arrest some of us here and take us back to Jerusalem in chains — me talk to him and risk getting arrested — you got to be kidding. No way!'* But as Ananias thought about it in terms of how there might be another side of this young man, he turned up his confidence and decided to reach for possibilities. In spite of the risk, he set out for Straight Street.

Although Ananias was guarded and suspicious when he met Paul, he soon found that the young Paul was no longer arrogant and defiant. To his surprise, he found a young man who was confused and troubled, but now humble and open to new ideas. Paul lis-tened as Ananias explained the reason he had decided to become a follower of the Way – living by the qualities of kindness and caring, instead of tradition and the absolutes of religious authority. It was a defining moment for Paul. He could see it now. The new Way was one of faith and service to people, not bondage to enslaving rules from the past. The new insights were transformational.

As Luke told about it in his metaphorical and dramatic style, he said it was like scales had fallen from Paul's eyes and he could see again. It was insight, understanding, seeing another point of view – a new self image. As Ananias talked to Paul about Jesus and his belief in a new order of caring and love, Paul began to change inside. He could see how he had been defending the old, instead of reaching for the new and better way. Ananias invited Paul to have dinner with him. As they sat and talked, Paul asked if he could be baptized into the new faith. After the baptism, Paul went with Ananias to the synagogue to tell the good news to others.

What a story! No wonder one of the best words in the Christian faith has been conversion. Change. Putting a new tomorrow beyond an old yesterday. Reaching past wrong and failure. Resetting dreams. Paul understood that kind of reprogramming identity and put that central concept in one of his letters to the church at Corinth. "When someone becomes a Christian he becomes a brand new person inside. He is not the same any more. A new life has begun!" (II Corinthians 5:17)

Damascus Road! It was quite a turning point in Paul's story. But, smooth sailing ahead now? Not at all. To the contrary, turbulence! And not far away. Before Paul left Damascus, some of the people who thought he had now utterly disavowed and betrayed Judaism, laid out a plot to kill him. Paul escaped by his friends letting him down over the city wall in a big basket.

From Damascus, Paul headed to Jerusalem to tell how he was a changed man. But the people in Jerusalem didn't believe him; thought it was a trap. Even the disciples didn't trust him. Then Barnabas arrived and began to tell that Paul was in fact a changed person. Even that, however, didn't ease the tension. When another plot was laid on his life by those who thought Paul had betrayed their religion. Some of Paul's friends "took him to Caesarea, and then sent him to his home in Tarsus." (Acts 9:30)

Back home again. What a journey since he left Tarsus such a short time ago to go off to college. Could he explain it to his parents? What now? Start making tents? Perhaps. No account is given as to how long he was there or what he did. We do know there was another time later when he fell back on tent making skills.

Meanwhile, the believers and followers of Jesus continued to grow. A lot of the people who had fled from Jerusalem during the persecution went to Antioch. The number of believers increased rapidly. It was there they adopted a new name for themselves. They called themselves Christians. The disciples of Jesus in Jerusalem knew about the growing number of converts in Antioch and sent Barnabas to help with the work there. That's when Barnabas thought about Paul, the one person, who above all others, was a personal example of the way a person could change and start a new life. So Barnabas went to Tarsus to hunt for him. When he found him, he told him how opposition had not stopped the movement. On the contrary, it was growing. 'Come with me to Antioch,' Barnabas pleaded. 'We need you there.' So Paul went with Barnabas to Antioch. They worked together for a full year before, Paul decided to go back to Jerusalem and then set out a series of travels as a missionary for the new faith he had discovered. Back and forth across the Mediterranean Sea, Paul went to Galatia, Macedonia, Philippi, Thessalonica, Athens, Corinth, Ephesus, and finally to Rome. He had founded churches in those places, often in the face of severe opposition and danger. But, did he regret his decision to chart his new role as ambassador to both Jews and Gentiles, bridging from a rigid religion of transcendence and adherence to authority, over to a faith of immanence, with openness to newness and change? Not at all! Let Paul tell of his own journey of trials and hardships as a world citizen.

"I have worked harder, been put in jail oftener, been whipped times without number, and faced death again and again. Five different times the Jews gave me their terrible thirty-nine lashes. Three times I was beaten with rods. Once I was stoned. Three times I was shipwrecked. Once I was in the open sea all night and the whole next day. I have traveled many weary miles and have been often in great danger from flooded rivers, and from robbers." (II Corinthians 11: 23 – 26) The list goes on, and he apologized for telling about his troubles, when in fact, they had advanced the cause to which he had devoted himself.

Why was he so devoted and persistent? He said, "So I run straight to the goal with purpose in every step ... Like an athlete I punish my body, treating it roughly, training it to do what it should, not what it wants to. Otherwise I fear that after enlisting others for the race, I myself might be declared unfit and ordered to stand aside." (I Corinthians 9:26 – 27)

When Paul was in jail, and couldn't visit the churches he had founded on his journeys around the rim of the Mediterranean Sea, he wrote letters and sent them by young men, some of whom became leaders in churches. As an unintended sideline, those letters were saved and through them, Paul tells his own story. In his story, instead of measuring by little short-term ups and downs, he measured by long term goals, achievable only as one perseveres beyond adversity and setbacks.

When some of the disciples claimed they were more credentialed in representing the faith because they had actually seen Jesus, while Paul had only met him in a vision, Paul countered by saying that he had seen Jesus in a higher sense – that he had met the metaphorical Christ on Damascus Road, and that, instead of being chosen, he had made his own choice to be a follower. He could speak firsthand about finding a new beginning beyond an old ending.

Paul's choice represented and expanded the concept of faith as being universal and inclusive of all people, a dynamic, open-ended faith, instead of just Jewish religion. Fast forward that understanding to our molecular age and we find it's parallel in the Big Ten Universal Qualities that can be chosen by anyone, anywhere, beyond all boundaries.

In a letter to the church in Rome, Paul listed the leading-edge humanitarian qualities he embraced as his pathway to being a world citizen.

> Don't just pretend that you love others; really love them. Hate what is wrong. Stand on the side of the good. Love each other with brotherly affection and take delight in honoring each other. Never be lazy in your work but serve the Lord enthusiastically.
>
> Be glad for all God is planning for you. Be patient in trouble, and prayerful always. When God's children are in need, you be the one to help them out. And get into the habit of inviting guests home for dinner, or if they need lodging for the night.
>
> If someone mistreats you because you are a Christian, don't curse him; pray that God will bless him. When others are happy, be happy with them. If they are sad, share their sorrow. Work happily together. Don't try to act big. Don't try to get into the good graces of important people, but enjoy the company of ordinary folks. And don't think you know it all!
>
> Never pay back evil for evil. Do things in such a way that everyone can see you are honest clear through. Don't quarrel with anyone. Be at peace with everyone, just as much as possible. Be friends, never avenge yourselves. . . Don't let evil get the upper hand but conquer evil by doing good. (Romans 12:9-18, 21)

By way of Damascus Road, the college student from Tarsus had become a world citizen. What he discovered was not a religion for a few people, but an open-ended faith for all people. It was a citizenship, defined not so much by where he had traveled in the world, as by the magnitude of the kingdom of heaven vision of the Master Teacher he met on Damascus Road.

CHAPTER TEN

Turning Point

Anyone, anywhere, and anytime,
can choose to make tomorrow better than yesterday.

THE EVENING CAMPFIRE COOKOUT ENDED WITH EVERYONE ROASTING marshmallows over the glowing coals. Now extra firewood had been put on the fire. In the glow of the light of the flames, the circle of grandchildren and Grandmother waited for Granddad to begin his story.

"Here we are, gathered down on the meadow again, down by the branch that meanders its way through this quiet meadow. It was your request. I certainly didn't object. Along with the farmhouse porch, this is one of my favorite places on the farm, especially when we can share it together as family. But, I know why you wanted to come down here again. You just wanted to be around the campfire and create some more, s'mores. Just kidding. I think you like walking down grassy roads to this meadow in this country setting as much as I do. Your grandmother and I truly treasure these times. You do us both a great honor. And I hope you like hearing my stories as much as I like telling them, because I have another wonderful story that I want to tell.

The story I am going to tell this evening is timeless, even though it bears all the marks of the time of Early Christianity, the story is about new beginnings beyond old endings, about resetting dreams, about signals to the mind that reshapes identity. Fast forward from this early story to our time and we find ourselves talking about how a person's life can be totally reprogrammed at turning point moments, where one's identity is redefined, and one's story redirected.

The story I am about tell is about Onesimus, but not just about him and his journey, but about resetting dreams in our digital, info-tech age.

So here we go, trekking along together on shared journey with a young man named, Onesimus, in the early days of Christianity. The reason his story has survived across the centuries is because an old letter was valued enough that it was kept. Then it was valued enough that it got included in the Bible, which, in turn, means it will still be kept for hundreds of years into the future as a story about new beginnings beyond old endings. It's a letter Paul wrote to Philemon on behalf of Onesimus.

It's a story that illustrates one of the Church's best words – conversion – new tomorrows. It is about how someone with a bad past can still build a good future. It's about turning points – about choices – about identity. Freedom from life's enslaving destructive forces in the past is only part of the equation. There is also the freedom to discover new images which open up creative forces that define a whole new future. So, let me connect some dots in history and geography to share with you the dramatic story of Onesimus.

Colossae was a little city on the banks of Lycus River. The people of Colossae had gathered in their new church building. It stood at the end of a street in ancient Colossae. And for the forty-six members of that church, it was a very important gathering. They were to have their first service in their new church building, and their special guest for the occasion was none other than Onesimus, Bishop of Ephesus.

No bishop of the early church was loved more than Onesimus. St. Ignatius of Antioch had written and circulated a letter giving a glowing description of his leadership. So, having Bishop Onesimus at their church in Colossae was very special. It was also important to Onesimus to be able to be there. The reason had to do with his own turning-point journey.

Bishops have a way of reminiscing when they go to some churches, and that's what Bishop Onesimus did when he went back to Colossae. Of course, he began by complimenting them on their new church.

"I can't tell you just how much it means for me to be the first person to preach in your new church. I commend you on your new church building. It's so nice and you will make it a special place for helping people find new tomorrows. I think you know, however, what an impact this church had on my life before you even had a building of any kind – back when you were meeting in the home of Philemon – back when Paul used to come by and spend several weeks at a time here. That's when I got my first glimpse of how we can turn the worst into the best, how even failures can lead to opportunity. Of course, I went through some strange journey in my life before I discovered that new source of guiding energy, and opened my life to a new understanding of freedom.

I remember that long journey down the river. And you are saying, 'Down the river? What do you mean by, down the river?' Well, I must tell you about that. I can still hear those oars dipping into the water as I let my mind go back to those nights I rowed my way down the river. Yes, it was night. And, yes, it was dark. Well, it was dark in two ways. I traveled down the river on a moonless night. But beyond that, it was dark in another way, for I was a run-away slave, seeking my freedom. I rowed down the Lycus River. It merged into the Meander River at Hierapolis. I was headed for the upbeat city of Ephesus, where I was going to begin a whole new life. I had money in my pocket and dreams in my head. It was a long shot, but I was ready for a long shot. You see, I was a slave of the man who founded this church, with the help of the Apostle Paul. I speak of Philemon. I belonged to Philemon in those days as his slave. I prepared and served meals to him and to Paul many times. I went out and invited people to come in for the services when Paul came by, and then I stood on the side of the room and listened. His sermons put wings on my soul, and I had that longing to be free. Only, then, I didn't understand all I needed to know about freedom. I thought if I could only get away from my owner I would be free. I hadn't learned the meaning of being "free in Christ" as Paul used to say – about having a new master and having a guiding purpose in life. So after Paul left Colossae, to go preach at other home churches, I decided to make a run for my freedom.

Now Philemon is here today even as I tell this. We all owe so much to him in this church. But I owe even more to him. I would say that I owe him some money, if it hadn't been for the fact that he forgave me of both my debt and my wrong long ago.

Philemon is sitting right down here in front of me and knows this story. But I am going to assume his permission, and take the liberty of telling it to you. I trust it will be a tribute of esteem to him as my very special friend, for that's how I mean it to be. You see, I stole some money from Philemon that night when I made my run for freedom. Not a pretty story for a bishop, but it's true, so I may as well tell it. Of course, any person who is trying to become somebody of worth and honor, has some part of the story he or she would like to forget. I knew where Philemon kept his money, so before I left, I just helped myself to it. It was a pretty good little sum. So that, plus the fact that I was a runaway slave, made it necessary for me to keep out of sight. That's the reason I went down the Lycus River at night. I stepped into a boat and turned quickly down stream. I dipped those oars quietly into the river all night long. When the first signs of daylight came, I pulled to the shore, in a densely wooded section, and hid out all day long. Wow, those were long days. You've heard of long nights; well, I had long days. I was glad when darkness came and I could get back on the river. It was night when I sailed into the Meander River and slipped past Hierapolis. Then in a couple more nights, I arrived in the city of Ephesus.

What I needed first was a change of clothes so I would not be identified as a slave. That was the first of Philemon's money I spent. Then, with my new clothes and a new feeling, I went for some good food and wine. And the good meals continued until my money ran out. When I stole some more money, that's when I got caught and landed in jail.

Now, there are some strange passages in this story, and this was one of them. Here I was seeking my freedom, but, instead of being free, I was in jail. But could you guess whom I saw in jail there in Ephesus? Yes, you could guess, for you have probably heard this part of the story. Of all the people I should meet in jail, it was Paul. The moment I saw him I knew him, and, even with my new clothes, he knew me. And the obvious question both of us had was, 'What on earth are you doing here?' I was ashamed to tell why I was there, but Paul wasn't at all ashamed to tell why he was there. He said he was in jail for preaching about Jesus, and counted it an honor to suffer persecution if the cause of Christ could be advanced.

Strange jail experience – it was like meeting an old friend. Of course, the credit for that goes to Paul, for he just kind of took me in like a child. He was like a father to me. I was soon released from jail, but I stayed in Ephesus and came back to the jail day after day to help Paul, bringing him food and warm clothes, and helping him with his letters to the churches.

Then one day, Paul said, 'Onesimus, what are you going to do about Philemon? You know, don't you, that sooner or later, he's going to find out where you are.'

I said, 'I don't know what to do. Oh, how I wish I could stay free! Do you know what I can do?'

And Paul said, 'Would you be willing for me to write a letter to Philemon and let you take it to him?'

Well, it didn't take long for me to be defensive about that. That's when I said, 'You mean, me take the letter to him and walk right back into slavery?'

'Well, not necessarily,' Paul said. 'You have set a new direction in your life. Now that you have become a Christian, I want to ask Philemon if he will receive you back, not as a slave, but as a brother in Christ.'

I never thought I would hear the oars dipping into the water of the Meander River and then the Lycus River again. But I did. This time the oars dipped many times to go a short distance as I trudged back upstream. At times, I couldn't believe myself for what I was doing, rowing right back into my master's hands. As the oars splashed, I thought and thought. I had seen slaves whipped for disobedience. I could be whipped in public for what I had done and then have to go right back into being a slave. Was I stupid? Why did I believe in Paul's appeal to Philemon?

I reached and felt in my pocket many times, making sure the letter Paul had written was still there. If it were not, I knew what I would do – turn that boat around and head back down the river. The letter was still there. I read what Paul had written to Philemon many times.

> Now I want to ask a favor of you... My plea is that you show kindness to my child Onesimus, whom I won to the Lord while here in my chains ... I really wanted to keep him here with me while I am in these chains for preaching the good news ... Perhaps you could think of it this way: that he ran away from you for a little while so that now he can be yours forever, no longer only a slave, but something much better – a beloved brother." (Philemon 8-16 Selected verses)

Finally I got back to where I had left earlier, and anchored my boat on the same shore I had left on my venture to freedom. As soon as I stepped out of the boat, I took out the letter and clutched it in my hand, as I walked up the hill from the river and then down the street to where Philemon lived.

It was early morning when I got there and Philemon was just coming up the street from his house. I walked up to him and said, 'Here.' I thrust the letter into his hand and said, 'Don't say a thing. Just read this. It's from Paul.' And when I said, 'It's from Paul,' his whole expression changed immediately.

Philemon took the letter and began to read. I waited in silence, almost like a criminal before a judge. And then he looked up with a big smile. With that letter in one hand, he reached out to embrace me and said, 'Welcome, my brother in Christ!' Tears rolled down my cheeks, and I knew first hand about the wonders of grace and the full measure of freedom.

As we walked toward the house, Philemon said, 'You're free, even as Paul asked, and the debt is fully forgiven. Don't ever think of it again. You are no longer my slave, but I still want you to do something for me, if you will – something you used to do when Paul was here. I want you to go out and invite the Christians to come to my house this evening to worship and to celebrate together.'

What a celebration service we had. I was welcomed! I was free as never before.

Some time later, Philemon said, 'Onesimus, I want you to do something special for me. I want you to go back to Ephesus and help Paul while he is in prison. He needs you more than I. And, in turn, I will be paying a debt I owe to him, for I am his child in the faith.'

When the time came for me to return to Ephesus, Philemon walked down to the river with me. And as I stepped into the boat, Philemon reached into his pocket and pulled out the letter Paul had written to him. He handed it to me and said, 'I want you to have this. Paul sent it to me, but really it's yours. You might say, it's your passport to freedom. God bless you. Give my greetings to Paul.'

The oars dipped into the water again as I went back to Ephesus. I helped Paul as long as he was there. Then I stayed in Ephesus and helped to carry on the work of the church. In time, I was chosen as a bishop. And now, after many years, I have the privilege of coming back here for this special and cherished occasion."

Bishop Onesimus waited a brief moment as he stood before the church in Colossae. He reached into his pocket and tenderly drew out a piece of paper, faded and worn. He looked down at it, almost with reverence. Then he looked up and said, "This is Paul's letter to Philemon. This is my passport to freedom. The years are passing, and I am getting older. I won't be here much longer. And, with my duties as Bishop of Ephesus, I may not get back here for a long time, if ever. So, while I am here, I want to leave this letter in your care and under your stewardship in this new church building. You can find a good place to keep it.

And now, Philemon, if you will grant me a high personal privilege, I would like to give the letter back to you, and through you, to the church, as a part of the many letters I helped Paul write to other churches. Perhaps some day the letters of Paul can be collected and circulated among all the churches.'

Philemon rose slowly and came forward. Bishop Onesimus walked out to meet him. He tenderly handed the letter to Philemon and said, 'My dear friend, would you do something for me? Would you take this letter in your hand and reach out your arms to embrace me, as you did many years ago, and would you be willing to say again what you said then, 'Welcome, my brother in Christ?'

The church kept the letter. It was included in a collection of Paul's letters and appears in the New Testament, under the title of Philemon. It's about turning points.

For Paul, a new beginning beyond an old ending happened on the road to Damascus. For Onesimus, that new beginning happened when he took a letter back up the river, as a bold new request of life.

From slave to bishop. Few of us will ever receive the historic recognition Onesimus received as Bishop of Ephesus, or have letters that are kept as long as his, but each of us can live out a faithful stewardship of the opportunities that come to us on our own turning points journey.

Some people achieve enough notoriety that someone else will write their life story. Some people keep a journal of their own life story, which I encourage each of you to do. Some people's life story will simply never be written, except as it is a part of the blended story of the earth family, but that is important.

The human story contains our story. Our own story may be like only drops of water in a river, but it is our highest stewardship responsibility. That story can show that we know how to turn tough journey into touchstone journey. It can show that we used our growing endowments in our new age of enlightenment to make a difference for good in spite of grave difficulties.

We can begin again – that's one of life's important affirmations to make at pivotal crossroads. Get fired from a job? We can find a new one. In a failed marriage? We can build new relationships. Failures in school? It's not the end of the road. Built up feelings of fear? We can get beyond them. Entangled in the bondage of crippling faith metaphors? We can learn new ways of thinking. There is always some better tomorrow beyond old yesterdays. We can find it. Old endings can be new beginnings. Will we ever get things perfect? Not likely. But we can keep on reaching beyond our failures for new levels of success? Maybe somebody will keep an old letter that tells how we put the past behind us and the future before us, as one of life's many new beginning places.

Jesus, Paul, and Onesimus, these are three leaders who defined humanity's kingdom of heaven vision as world citizens for new tomorrows. Updated as a reach for successful achievement, we can make the Big Ten Universal Qualities our overarching framework for our best future. That reach for the next level up in the progression of the human story has never been more important, or the rewards greater, than in our exciting digital, info-tech age. Anyone, anywhere, and anytime, can choose to make tomorrow better than yesterday. As an identity framework, these ten words overarch religion, politics, and culture to define our humanity in terms of the unparalleled potential we have to shape the future into distant new tomorrows. It's the new sacred!

In this progression, we are transitioning from a transcendence paradigm over to an immanence paradigm in which the quality of our humanity is more important than our technology. It's a call from the future. It's a place in the story where we can give our best dreams their best chance to happen.

It's my hope that these stories have awakened your best dreams. You have listened ever so respectfully to my outside Eden stories about pioneering forward beyond old endings to new beginnings for new tomorrows of nobility. I am honored and so very pleased that your grandmother and I have had this treasured time to share our dreams with our much loved grandchildren."

A brief moment of quietness followed, before Marsha broke the silence and out of her perspectives as an artist, said, "A painting freezes a moment in time. When people look at it they see, not only what was painted, but their own journey of similarities or contrasts. Granddad, the stories you have so graciously shared with us have become a benchmark painting with backdrops on yesterday out of which we now see tomorrow more clearly. Thank you, Grandmother and Granddad!"

Steve followed immediately. "Granddad, we all are immensely grateful to you for spring-boarding forward from that Young Writers Conference at the university to this farmhouse porch seminar for your grandchildren! You have helped us reset our identity by a call from the future, focused in the Big Ten Universal Qualities. More than ever now, we can see that what we plan to give to life becomes our request of life and the future we ask for. So thank you, Granddad and Grandmother, for this very special time to learn forward."

When all of the grandchildren began to applaud, Granddad held up his hands to indicate they need not applaud. "You are thanking us?" he said. "Your grandmother and I thank you for giving us these memorable and cherished moments in our own place in the story.

You have provided us an opportunity to pass the story-torch on down to a new generation.

And now, our little story seminar has come to an end here on the farmhouse porch, but we still get to share in one more special event. You already know that I have the privilege of speaking at the church of my boyhood at its annual Homecoming Day service. It will be a moment of immense pride if I can look down and see all of you there. I hope all of you have made plans to stay over and will be there to listen one more time."

Steve responded quickly. "Our plans are in place. Gladly, and with pride, we will be there!"

CHAPTER ELEVEN

Homecoming Sunday

You are the link that holds
yesterday's heritage and tomorrow's dreams together.

The Magic Word

THE WHITE FRAME NEW HOME CHURCH OF GRANDDAD'S BOYHOOD
had been replaced by a brick church with a tall steeple. Granddad
didn't know, but he hoped they had kept the bell from the old
church and put it in the new steeple so that it could still send out
that special sound out across the countryside on Sunday mornings.
He had loved to hear it ring when he was a boy, and would love to
hear it again on Homecoming Sunday. He was delighted that Steve
had spoken so enthusiastically for all of his cousins, 'We'll be there.'
Now they too, might get to hear that old bell ring!

After Granddad was kindly, evenly glowingly, presented as a
favorite son of New Home Church, he stepped up to the pulpit
with a respect so treasured that it was as though he were receiving
the Nobel Prize. As he began his presentation, it was obvious that

he felt a measure of fondness and great respect for the church and its pulpit. Cordially, and with tenderness in his voice, he began.

"It's your annual Homecoming Day, but it's more than that for me. You may not fully realize just how special it is for me to stand here today. I remember standing behind the old pulpit in the old white frame church of my boyhood days, imagining myself being the preacher. I didn't quite realize how prophetic it was, or how that role would get extended into, not only being a minister, but also a professor, metaphorical philosopher, and writer. I treasure this moment now, many years later. Mrs. Kelly and I also treasure having all our family here, including all our three children and grandchildren.

Do you know what our grandchildren have been doing this week? They have been listening to me tell stories on the farmhouse porch, where my mother used to read stories to me from a farm magazine when I was a boy, stories that helped build dreams that have lead my future. I hope our children and grandchildren will return to that old porch in their minds many times and turn the metaphorical stories we shared together into metaphors for their own journey dreams. Whatever tomorrow may be like, we all need "farmhouse porches" where we keep resetting our dreams.

Upon the invitation of your young minister and homecoming committee, I have been given a very high privilege of speaking here today. I do it with great respect for all those who have made this church such a good church and a vital part of this caring community across so many years. You are the link that holds yesterday's heritage and tomorrow's dreams together. I deeply appreciate the work that goes forward now as a new generation is leading the way. Thank you for giving me this very special privilege of being a part of this continuing legacy. I am greatly honored.

Your bulletin gives the title of my message, along with a listing of the ten words which define what I call, the Big Ten Universal Qualities – ten qualities that cross all boundaries in our global family and define a faith that leads to an open-ended future. I will focus on one of the Big Ten defining words, with a title of, "The Magic Word." Maybe you are already guessing which of the ten is the magic word.

The ten words that I call the Big Ten Universal Qualities are words we can use wherever we live and relate to each other. If you care to look at your bulletin, you can follow the words as I name them. They are kindness, caring, honesty, respect, collaboration, tolerance, fairness, integrity, diplomacy, and nobility. If we can live by these words, we will pass life's most important tests and create a story of successful achievement. In fact, if we can live by the first word, we get an "A" just for that. So, what is the magic word? It's kindness.

Homecoming. It's a time when we get to meet with old friends. Beyond remembering the past, it is also a time to touch the growing edge of the future and build new friendships.

So, I need the help of some new friends. I have recruited two young friends as my helpers. So, 'Brent and Julia, would you please come up now and read a few very select words for us?'

Julia will be reading Philippians 4:8 from the New English Bible. Let's listen, as Julia reads.

"And now, my friends, all that is true, all that is noble, all that is just and pure, all that is lovable and gracious, whatever is excellent and admirable, fill your thoughts with these things."

Now, Brent, would you please read for us, Ephesians 4:32? It's short, but important. Very important. Listen.

"Be . . . kind to one another."

'Julia and Brent, thank you for being my very special new friends here. You may not remember what I say here today, but the chances are good that you will remember that I asked you to read today's lessons as new friends. You have helped us think about kindness.'

I hope you won't mind my taking a moment to turn back the clock and reflect on earlier times. There's so much I would like to say, but I will try to keep it in a reasonable time frame before we gather around the table for a grand homecoming dinner. Being here on Homecoming Day makes me remember those homecoming dinners we had when I was a boy, and could hardly wait for the preacher to finish his long winded sermon so we could have our homecoming dinner under the trees. Today we will gather in a fellowship hall, but in those early days, we gathered under the big oak trees. One of the things I remember so vividly is that someone would buy two new "number two" wash tubs, put in big chunks of ice and fill those tubs with lemonade. There was a new dipper in each tub. We could fill our cups as many times as we wanted. And was that lemonade ever good? It was not just good, it was gooood! But I don't want to say too much now about those grand dinners, lest you get so hungry and thirsty before I even get started that you won't hear what I have to say.

I hope my message will be openly received by all of you, but I will be especially pleased if Carl Morton finds it to be an extension of his progressive thinking. 'Carl, I see you in the audience and I am pleased that you are here.' Carl Morton is one of the persons I remember so respectfully from my early days. He was so kind. And he was intellectually brilliant. He was a young science teacher at the high school. Not only was he one of my heroes; he was highly respected by all the people of the church. He helped this church have an open mind to newness, and that is a very special gift to bring to a church and rural community. Not every church is open to the progression of knowledge for a molecular understanding of who we are in our digital, info-tech age, but there's a good chance this church is open to accepting new paradigms. Much of the thanks for that belongs to Carl Morton, who put his faith together with the science he taught in school, and the kindness he showed to all of us when we were young. Carl bridged the gap between the generations.

There are three generations of the Kelly family represented here today. I represent the generation that will pass off the stage, but not as quickly as only a few years ago. Our average life-expectancy is moving toward eighty, and with the benefits of new biotech medicine, that may soon move up to one hundred, and beyond. So, you will have my age group with you for a while longer. The demographic that I represent is well represented here today. As I look across the audience I see more people in this "graying" category than in the next successive category, their children, or the next category down from that, their grandchildren, who are beginning to take a significant place in the story.

So as the progression goes on there has been, and will be, lots of change. What shall we do about all this change? How can we turn change into opportunity to advance the greatest age the human family has ever known? Let me talk about that opportunity in terms of a vision call from the future.

First, a vision call from the future includes using the accumulated resources in the progression of our civilization up to this time so they lead to a higher humanity. It is time to invest this heritage from yesterday into a bold, leading-edge dream vision of our best tomorrow. We are making progress in our human story, but we have not arrived yet. We can expect to live longer, and that is our extended opportunity to be "kind to one another" across multiple generations. We have the special opportunity to make all the qualities of the Big Ten Universal Qualities such a part of the way we live and use our resources, that each successive generation can be celebrated as the successive Big Ten Generation. In turn, we all can leave a legacy of turning old endings into new beginnings so that each new tomorrow becomes better than yesterday. Our opportunity is to live as close to fulfilling a utopian dream as we can for our place in the story.

Second, a vision call from the future includes a call to think ahead, and build scenarios that project our best future as our request of life. It's a call to dream ahead and live such a quality life that we become that model person we would like to meet if we were meeting ourselves.

Third, a vision call from the future includes working alongside robots and finding new ways to do what robots cannot do. Robots will become ubiquitous work-place partners in our future, and an invisible part of our lifestyle. They may even be the playmates of our grandchildren and great grandchildren. Robots will be everywhere. But they can't do everything. In fact, they cannot do one very important thing. Robots can't tell stories from yesterday that become identity metaphors for new tomorrows. They can't represent the kindness and understanding we can give. That's our own going opportunity, no matter how much robots change the way we live. We can always be kinder than a robot. And because we may live longer than any generation before us, that only gives a longer place in the story to be "be kind to one another." So we have lots of opportunity left.

Fourth, a vision call from the future includes a call to a higher humanity by making the Big Ten Universal Qualities the identity markers that define who we are.

Two major paradigms have framed the way people have seen the world across many generations. One of those is transcendence. It's about the way to live as defined by a God of ultimate authority, above and beyond our world. It's modeled in the book of The Revelation of John, most often just called "Revelations," where God has it all figured out for a final wrap up of the human story, with some going off to paradise, but most going down to history's fiery wastebasket.

The other backdrop that frames the way people see the world is immanence. In that worldview the responsibility for the future is up to its people. It is modeled by the book of Proverbs, in which, one little proverb after another, Solomon asked the young people of his time to run scenarios of their own future choices – to look ahead and figure out which choices lead to something bad, and which ones lead to the best life one can find, and then make the smart choices that lead to that good, wise, rewarding, and wholesome life.

It's this later approach which aligns with the tremendous potential we hold in our hands in our time in history. It's the retiree generation that has done so much to add to the accumulation of knowledge. It's the middle generation that is now advancing our potential in our business and educational systems, with the help of computers and digital communication. And it's the new grandchildren generation that is bringing in the information-age, with its growing molecular and knowledge-based understanding of who we are and what we can do on a scale of unparalleled potential. And their children will be the ones who really take hold of the steering wheel and guides us the next level where the information-age merges into the neuroscience and biotech-robotic age. And it's in these blended techno-human ages, that all of us have such a big opportunity. We can integrate the increasingly important qualities of the Big Ten Universal Qualities into the identity markers we measure by, and try to live up to, at new levels day by day! It's time for an identity shift from transcendence to immanence!

The age of transcendence is fading. The age of immanence is rising. More and more we know the Solomon thesis is right – that the future is up to us – that the qualities we plan to live by reset our dreams. Solomon put forth his wisdom viewpoints in short little proverbs, anecdotes, and scenarios to show that, what we plan to give to life becomes our request of life. As a kind of update on Solomon's proverbs, we now have the word tools of the Big Ten Universal Qualities as an overarching identity framework to guide our request of life.

For Solomon it was the age of immanence, indicating that the future is up to us. More than ever, it is time to make this the age of immanence. We bear the responsibility to enter those choices which become powerful pacesetters for our best future. Those who are doing research in neuroscience are learning that the brain is plastic and changes itself. It can reprogram its guidance signals to lead us to be the Big Ten Generation.

The fifth vision call from the future is a call to the church. This is the greatest age the church has ever known to make a knowledge-based faith and the Big Ten Universal Qualities the guiding markers to define its mission. This call to the church would honor its mission to our age better if it represented the way Jesus lived more than the way he died.

Instead of a cross on the altar, if we had a figure of Jesus teaching from the mountainside, with people standing below listening, that central focus would celebrate learning as the pathway to a great tomorrow. It would represent immanence and humanitarian service, rather than transcendence and captivity to tradition.

When we read the story of Jesus, as presented by his biographers, the worldview that shows up most in his teachings is not transcendence, but immanence It was summarized in his vision of a "kingdom of heaven on earth." It was a vision Jesus dared to live by and can be represented best by showing him as the Master Teacher of the ages. Updated to our time, it is extended by a knowledge-based faith that honors science, technology, and the Big Ten Universal Qualities as the benchmark we measure by for our place in the story.

With great respect for the Master Teacher, when John presented Jesus in his biography, he wrote, "Early in the morning he came again into the temple, and all the people came unto him; and he sat down, and taught them." John 8:2 KJV

In my boyhood days, I was at this church every Sunday. Every Sunday morning of my early life, my parents loaded my two older brothers and me into a thirty-five model Ford car and drove three miles to the big, white, weatherboard New Home Church for Sunday School. What I remember about those early years, is that my boyhood Sunday School teachers were such kind and caring persons. Fundamentalism may have defined their theology, but it was their human qualities of kindness, courtesy, patience, cordiality, graciousness, and congenial hospitality that I felt, and now remember most. Their qualities overarched their religion as a re-freshing faith. They were among my early heroes.

My parents were quality people. When I go out to the farm to do some of my writing, it puts me back into that context of respect. I write in the farmhouse where my grandparents and parents lived, and where I grew up. They were honorable people. My grandparents helped build the old white church. Their lifestyle modeled being caring, helpful, and kind. I am greatly indebted to them. I hope my being here in this pulpit today is a tribute of honor to them and extends their legacy.

Theology tends to overemphasize transcendence and worshiping God, somewhere in a distant heaven, and tends to underemphasize immanence, down here where we live day by day. We need to reverse that, and put immanence at the peak of our faith.

Why is kindness the magic word? You can be a millionaire and still be poor if you don't have kindness. Or you can be economically depressed, but be rich, if you have kindness. Kindness is the quality that turns the light on for all the other nine qualities and guides them to higher levels. So one of life's greatest honors is to be known as one who fulfills the axiom, 'Be kind to one another.' No badges need to be pinned on your lapel. People will know it already, and you will know it.

The people who take care of the farm have a special kind of genuineness that makes it a pleasure to work together with them . They live out the qualities of the Big Ten as an extension of their faith. The church they attend has no cross on the altar. The emphasis of their faith is on immanence – on living out the qualities modeled by Jesus as the great Teacher. It's a faith that comes alive anew in daily living right there on the farm, as they plant and harvest the corn, cut the grass, roll the hay, pick the grapes, gather the persimmons, and fish the lake. They may not know the meaning of a word like scenario, but the way they see the world indicates they know how to live by the proverbs of

Solomon, which ask each person to learn how to look down the road and see the consequences of good and bad choices, then be smart enough to choose the good. They know how to extend the vision of the Teacher, updated in the Big Ten Universal Qualities by being 'kind to one another.'

What if we made, not just kindness, but all of the words of the Big Ten Universal Qualities into the working word tools we use each day to shape our identity? What if we simply choose one of those qualities as the "Quality-of-the Day," and apply it all day long as the one quality we try to make real? It's something each of us can do in a one–person clinical trial. And when we try and fail, we know what to do, get up and dust the dust off and try again. We know that failure can be a part of learning – a way to self-correct and reset our dreams. Over time, when we persist in sending the identity markers of the Big Ten Universal Qualities to the brain it will guide us to new tomorrows.

We live in the most dynamic age the human family has ever known, with potential to reach beyond our best yesterday for even greater tomorrows. This makes our time in history, the most dynamic age the human family has ever known to reset our dreams for the digital, info-tech age!

My message has come to an end, but I have a question. What if that old bell from yesterday could ring today? What if we could ring it now, not only announce our Homecoming Dinner, but to ring a call to dream our best dreams and give them their best chance to happen?

So, let me ask. 'Carl Morton, do you know what happened to that bell from the old white frame church?'"

Carl stood up and said, 'Yes, Dr. Kelly, I know. We all know. It's in the bell tower of our new steeple.'

"Then, let me ask another question. 'Could someone ring that bell now? My guess is, that the children here are as eager to hear it ring now as I was when their age. I am guessing they are ready to say, 'Let it ring!'

Listen. It's ringing now, DINNNG…DOOONG. DINNNG… DOOONG. But I hear it saying more than that. It's saying, KINNND…NESSS. . . KINNND…NESSS. . . KINNND… NESSS…"

SEQUELS: *New Tomorrows, Apple Blossom Time,*
The Future We Ask For, A Place In The Story,
Eagles View Mountain, Sunrise Dreams, The New Sacred.